THE HAPPY SOUL INDUSTRY

THE
HAPPY SOUL INDUSTRY

STEFFAN POSTAER

Portland • Oregon
INKWATERPRESS.COM

For Susan

"Advertisers are the interpreters of our dreams – Joseph interpreting for the Pharaoh. Like the movies, they infect the routine futility of our days with purposeful adventure. Their weapons are our weaknesses: Fear, ambition, illness, pride, selfishness, desire, ignorance. And these weapons must be kept as bright as a sword."

– E. B. White

"It doesn't get any better than this."

– Slogan, Old Milwaukee Beer

ONE

P ICTURE serenity. The atmosphere was fluid. Light shimmered and broke apart as if through liquid, glowing from the center, spreading outward, like on a child's drawing of the sun or as petals would on a pink and golden flower. Here was God now, materializing in a phantasmal swirl, its movement and pattern forming Her gown and hair. And She: An elegant female. Statuesque. A mortal would think She resembled the Statue of Liberty.

God waved Her right hand, and in the subsequent spray of light an angel, David Angelo, appeared. They were having a conversation, one begun earlier. "People are not responding to the message anymore," She said to David. "They don't appear to be motivated. We're losing them."

The angel did not like it when God expressed discontent. He knew it was born of concern for Her flock but it troubled him. He felt an acute sense of sorrow. David attempted to compose himself. God was, after all, all around him.

"Faith is elusive to many people but we must depend on it as we always have," David said to Her quietly. It was all he could say. The world was in disarray but hadn't it always been? Non-believers abounded. Why was God so upset about it now?

The Lord answered. "Faith is a component of an elaborate and archaic plan. To have people trust in something they cannot see; it was supposed to strengthen our relationship but-"

"But it does!" David retorted compassionately. He did not mean to interrupt Her but at the same time he wasn't afraid of speaking up. He was never afraid of God.

"No, David. It *did*," She replied, smiling warmly. The Lord cleared a place in the mist, revealing various earthly artifacts. They hovered before them, rotating slowly to the fore. Many of them David recognized: A gold Buddha. The star of David. A crucifix. But others were not familiar. He reached for a doll made of tightly wound reeds, a woman, her arms and legs outstretched as if in rapture.

"One of my favorites," said God, sensing his wonder. "She symbolizes me as Mother Earth, which, by the way, is a role I have always appreciated. Many Native Americans believed in her. Few do now."

David let go of the figurine, watching it vanish with the others. He turned.

And God was before him, Her features resembling those of the wicker doll. She closed her eyes and, just as quickly, became Jesus Christ, smiling beatifically.

Instinctively, David crossed himself.

God's muscles contorted. She grew larger and ever more masculine. The robe she was donning turned into a loincloth, wrapping around her massive girth, and transforming her yet again.

"All hail Zeus!" God bellowed. She cast a fiery lightning bolt toward the pink and blue horizons of Heaven. It exploded like a skyrocket, followed by the requisite clap of thunder.

David shuddered in awe of God's display. He well remembered

Zeus from his childhood schoolbooks. As a boy he had been fond of the Greek gods; they reminded him of superheroes, wrestlers.

"My myths were very popular in their day, dear boy. But what day is it now?" God asked, reading David's mind. She was herself again, mortal looking, save for the rapidly changing colors of her hair. Just then it was red turning fiery orange. She continued: "Unfortunately these myths became violent and corrupt. To some, symbols of fear. The very opposite of what I intended. And that's the problem with them all. They've either become irrelevant like our friend Zeus, or their meaning has warped. Mother Earth turning into a witch."

"Granted, your virtues are difficult to maintain, my Lord. Yet, we must keep trying." David spoke evenly. All in Heaven were aware of the dilemma. Icons of goodness were subject to false interpretation and worse: vile degradations, the situation bedeviling the nation of Islam, a current abhorrent example. Even God's best angels couldn't find a way to bring Arab and Jew together. Jerusalem had gone from Earth's holiest city to one of its bloodiest. There was so much shame in the world. Evil was a plague.

"Indeed, we must keep trying," said the Lord, bristling at the images of blasphemy and blood. Then She brightened. "But that is why you are here, dear boy! I have a program in mind. Something new and different." She'd inadvertently floated away from the angel and quickly righted herself in front of him.

"*New and different?*" These were not words one heard very often in Heaven. And certainly not coming from God.

"I'm afraid our image is wanting. We must evolve. Burning bushes and parting waters. Those were but cheap parlor tricks compared to what they do in modern cinema."

"Cheap tricks! But those are some of your most beloved-"

"Tricks." God clapped Her hands resolutely.

When she opened them they were inside an earthly temple, ancient and dreary, primarily lit by candles. David could barely make out an old rabbi working near the back. Muttering, the scholar leaned over a massive and decrepit book, unaware of the visitors.

God whispered. "He's attempting yet another translation of the make-believe scroll we planted in the desert."

"Make-believe?"

"More so-called proof of my existence," sighed God. "Even if it were an accurate accounting it wouldn't make a difference."

Confused, David shook his head. Why were they here anyway?

"Look around you, David. This place of worship is falling apart." She waved her hands, causing pigeons to shuffle in the eaves. "More scribbles from a cave will not effect change. Why people look for miracles in mud puddles and under rocks is endlessly frustrating to me. Even when I bring a statue to tears or provide a girl with stigmata, nobody cares, nobody is listening."

"That's not fair, my Lord," implored David. "People *do* care."

"Just the wounded and obsessed," she said sympathetically. "The vast majority write it off as poppycock. And I'm inclined to agree with them. Dead Sea scrolls...The Shroud of Turin. Give me a break! The genuine articles are as futile to our mission as the fakes. I mean, look at that poor rabbi. He slaves away on some decaying manuscript and the seats here go empty. Where is his congregation? Where are the faithful? We need to do something..."

"New and different?"

"Exactly."

Taking a seat, God removed a worn copy of the Old Testament from the pew in front of them. "I always preferred the New."

"Both are fine documents, my Lord."

"Fire and brimstone....Wine from water....The Ten Commandments....Forgive my repetition but this sort of thing motivates no one. Not anymore. In order to inspire goodness we've got to improve our image, which means, dare I say it, we need better copy!"

"Copy?" David asked tentatively. "Isn't that a term for advertising text, the kind one finds in a newspaper?" Tenderly, he leafed through pages from the Old Testament.

"Yes it does," God spoke, becoming excited. "And maybe we'll do some television commercials as well."

When David died television was in its infancy, like radio with pictures, barely real. Surprised by the idea, he clucked his tongue. The old rabbi felt it as he would a kiss on the neck. *The butterfly effect.* Agitated, he looked around, but seeing nothing unusual returned to his volumes.

"Are you suggesting we... *advertise?*"

God was floating again, lost in thought. "I took counsel with some of the more illustrious in the field. Barnum and Bailey you know. But I also spoke to the famed copywriter, William Bernbach. With his campaign for Volkswagen cars, he single-handedly turned advertising into popular culture. Anyway, they all thought marketing Heaven would be a capital idea!"

David smiled, his first, both at God's notion and at the way she employed British colloquialisms like "capital idea." Accents had been her invention and English was her favorite. "So, is your plan to have these departed gentlemen put together an ad campaign?"

Distracted by defamatory graffiti on the outside wall of the synagogue, God removed it instantly with a brush of her hand. "Not exactly. I also had an illuminating chat with one of our newer entrants from the advertising profession. Have you met Mr. Ogilvy? He shares your first name."

The angel shook his head.

"David had a big ego but in his day he was a marketing genius. He founded Ogilvy & Mather in New York. While there he wrote much of the copy for The Man in the Hathaway Shirt. It was his idea putting an eye patch on that fellow. All very successful."

David had no clue what God was talking about, having died before Ogilvy's advertising creation. "And what ideas, pray tell, were given to you?"

"Well," said God, "P.T. Barnum suggested we put together a show of hellish abominations and tour the country. 'Scare folk into servitude by showing them the consequences.' He called it the 'Freak-show From Hell.'"

David shuddered. "That's a ghastly idea."

"But at least it wasn't a bag of rocks like Mr. Ogilvy's suggestion." God seldom employed sarcasm. It humanized Her greatly. "He recommended we take a more conservative approach. That long and earnest copy would turn the tide. He even offered to write it." God rolled her eyes. "Long and earnest copy? My heavens, we already have *that*. The last thing we need around here is another sermon." She extended her arms, implicating the decayed temple.

Sheepishly, David returned the Old Testament to its rack. "So, who's going to revise our *copy*? Make it new and different?" He had a hard time referring to the rhetoric of truth and beauty as copy. And he still didn't know God's plan. He stared at his sandals. Meanwhile, the rabbi mumbled a Yiddish hymn, not prettily.

"Interestingly enough," God responded, "Mr. Ogilvy harped on what he called a 'creative boutique.' He claimed these small agencies possessed a very high caliber of creative talent but that they tended to be full of themselves and were only interested in getting attention. Frankly, I think one of these so-called boutiques would be perfect for us."

"What about Madison Avenue? Isn't that where the most famous advertising agencies reside?"

"Please! We might as well ask the Vatican for help!" God paused, giving it more thought. "However, if you're so inclined you may visit a New York agency. You have my blessing. As our new Vice-President of Marketing, it's your call anyway."

David panicked. It hit him: The Lord wants me to find an advertising agency for...Heaven. "Oh God, not me!" he pleaded. "I mean I hardly think I'm the right choice. I used to sell insurance after all. And that was years ago. With all due respect, shouldn't you find someone more...more appropriate?"

God couldn't help but laugh. From Her glee, dozens of the expired candles about the temple lit up. Not surprisingly, this caused the rabbi to fall to his knees in prayer. But God was too preoccupied to notice. "Don't sell yourself short, David. You're far more suited for the task than you think." She was grinning like a mortal. "You knew the modern world at its most chaotic. You were in your prime at the turn of the twentieth century so you experienced the first autos, planes and phones, even our first global war. David, you are more than capable of navigating Earth now. I think you'll even enjoy it. "

The angel knew he was not getting out of this. He bit his lip, something he hadn't done since living. It wasn't that he was unwilling to do the Lord's work, but could he? "How will I know what to say? Or even how to behave?"

Said God: "As my emissary, you will have many skills. But more importantly, you will have me. You need only to ask me for help, as you always have, through prayer. And remember, dear boy, everything happens for a reason. There are no coincidences."

Feeling dizzy, David steadied himself on a pew. "I hope I won't let you down."

"You seldom have," responded the Lord. "That is why you are here."

"Where will I be going?"

God winked. "The City of Angels, of course." She reassured him with a squeeze to his shoulder. "But first we'll need to brush you up. Get you a suitable wardrobe. A haircut."

David nodded self-consciously. He hadn't thought about his hair in years.

God put Her hands together and once again they were in Heaven, its blue and pink sky feathering above like cotton candy.

TWO

"F UCK me." Vernon Night struggled to maneuver the new Path Maker XL into his impossibly small parking space. The architect who built this place should be shot, Vernon groused, as he twisted the leather-clad steering wheel. Vernon routinely made three cuts but this morning he was already on his fifth. It pissed him off he had to struggle, considering he was the goddamn President. The sign over his head said so: **Vernon Night, President.** Now it mocked him. As did his partner's car, which sat on top of the yellow line designating each spot. Vernon fantasized about ramming Barry's silver coupe back where it belonged. Instead he turned his vehicle's engine off. Exhaled. Resentments were too complicated to deal with in a parking garage, especially at eight o'clock on a Monday morning. He opened the door, or tried to, but Barry's car was still too close. The door went only inches.

"Fuck me!" Vernon restarted his vehicle and made another attempt negotiating the space. Unfortunately, it brought him in even tighter. He'd quit smoking three months ago and he ached for a cigarette now. Exasperated, he turned on the CD player: The Beatles' *Norwegian Wood*, a calming tune if ever there was one. He practiced the deep breathing exercise his shrink had taught him. But that didn't work either. It felt more like he was holding his breath. Then the CD skipped.

"Fuck meeee."

Upstairs Mila prepared Vernon's coffee: three parts Starbucks Morning Blend and one part Seattle's Best Hawaiian Mocha. Vernon could tell the difference so she had to get it right. But, alas, they were out of fresh cream! All she could find were those little creamer cups left over from a business meeting. Normally, that would not do but she'd overslept this morning (last night's Humanology meeting went longer than usual) and had been unable to stop at the store.

She considered going online for cream but even FoodFast.com wouldn't be fast enough. Instead Mila opened and poured as many of the portable creamers as she could into Vernon's Silver Slipper award. (The Slippy had been awarded to CN&W for its Taco-Laco talking dog campaign, and even though Vernon downplayed the prize in front of others, he was immensely proud of it.) Here the non-dairy creamers would pass muster. Vernon would never question the contents of his beloved Silver Slipper.

Mila brought the coffee service into his office. She couldn't help rolling her eyes at the black and white portrait of Vernon's wife, that is, his estranged wife. Regardless of how that eventually played out, Mila regretted having slept with Vernon.

She opened his calendar. Vernon was a busy man this week. Two CEOs were coming to call Wednesday and yet another dot-com on Thursday. He had his shrink on Tuesday and the agency's 10th anniversary party that night. Unfortunately for him (he'd undoubtedly be hung over), Tae-Bo was the following morning. Mila searched for an opening to accommodate the Happy Soul Industry, whatever that was. Mr. Angelo had called late on the previous Friday. This being

L.A. everybody but she had gone home for the weekend. She needed to get back to him as quickly as possible. God forbid a new business prospect went to another agency because of a scheduling bug. She wrote down Happy Soul at ten and returned to her desk.

The Happy Soul client resided at the Four Seasons in Beverly Hills. Mila knew the number by heart. She'd just been on the phone with them regarding the anniversary party. Mr. Angelo had a suite, which meant, along with good taste, he possessed a considerable expense account. Mila was relieved. CN&W had recently been scorched by yet another flash-in-the-pan dot-com. "The check's in the email" was a phrase a resident copywriter had coined in their honor. A fat cat for a client would make a nice change.

An impeccably courteous woman put her on hold. Vivaldi's *Four Seasons* played through her headset. Mila didn't make the connection but she recognized the song from a movie, or was it a commercial?

While waiting, Mila reminisced about the night she and Vernon had fooled around at the famous hotel. They were both married at the time, not yet unhappily, but wanting something new and naughty in their lives: Vernon because he wasn't getting *any* at home, Mila because she never got *enough*. Moral and ethical issues aside, the arrangement certainly had had that going for it. Until Vernon screwed it up: One Friday afternoon, buzzed on champagne and orgasm, he'd opined the reason she needed a big-time executive in her life was to validate it. This became the exact moment Mila stopped fucking him. They still got along, maybe even better than before. But the affair, free of consequences, was over. As for Mila, she renewed her marital vows and got herself a vibrator.

"I'm sorry," the polite voice on the phone said. "Mr. Angelo is not responding. Would you like me to ring the pool?"

"No, that's okay," replied Mila. "It's cold outside. He won't be swimming. I'll just leave a message."

"Very well. Have a nice day and thank you for calling the Four Seasons in Beverly Hills."

Mila left a brief message suggesting a meeting time, including the agency's general number as well as Vernon's private line. Mila was pleased with herself. She liked to choreograph most communications ahead of time in order to avoid mistakes. Mila had come a long way since joining Humanology.

"I NEED YOU to write a memo." Vernon stood before her, appearing frazzled despite his black Armani turtleneck and gray sport coat.

"And good morning to you too, Vern." It's not that Mila hated being his administrative assistant. But she deserved more respect. *A lot more.* She retaliated. "That outfit makes you look like William Shatner. Pre Boston Legal."

"Funny. I was trying for the other guy. The one who always gets laid." He managed a grin. The snarky rapport was par for the course.

She handed Vernon his coffee, following him back into his office. "How was your weekend? Did you and *Air-y* manage to get through it in one piece?"

He resented the question. Including her catty use of the name Airy. "As a matter of fact, Erin and I saw a movie. Now about that memo…"

"Which one?" Mila admired her nails.

"The one you are about to begin writing." Still ticked from the parking spot fiasco, Vernon was in no mood to chitchat with his secretary, let alone about his weekend with the wife. *He was going to write the memo from Hell.*

Of course, ignoring Mila was not the way to handle Mila. "I meant," and here she paused for effect, "which *movie* did you see?" She enunciated every syllable.

"I don't remember the title. Something about dinosaurs."

Mila scoffed. "I don't believe you." And as if it mattered: "Who was in it?"

Vernon shut his eyes. The Xanax he'd taken in the car wasn't working. He wanted a cigarette. "I don't know. A triceratops."

Reluctant to admit she didn't know what a triceratops was, Mila halted her interrogation. Sighing: "Okay, so what's your memo about this time?"

Excellent. They were done playing games. Vernon began orating: "Effective immediately those of you with *ordinary* cars MUST use extreme caution when parking next to those of us with *extraordinary* cars. No wait," he interrupted himself, "change the first part to read those of you with *ordinary* cars MUST park on the lower level, out of the way... *period*."

"Don't you mean out of *your* way, period?" chimed Barry from the doorway. He walked in, not quite done. "The problem isn't your parking spot, Vernon, it's that behemoth you drive." He grinned, loving to needle his partner almost as much as flirting with Mila. He leaned over and gave her a kiss. "Hi sweetie. Miss me?"

Barry Fine made 300-plus a year but still came to work unkempt, in ripped jeans. Had he even showered? The bed-head was obvious. He was also the Executive Creative Director of the agency and, although his name was not on the door, a partner. He had the same rank as Vernon, which drove Vernon crazy.

"That *behemoth* happens to be our biggest client's best-selling SUV. It wouldn't hurt you to be seen in one."

"Oh yes it would."

Mila could watch her bosses spar all morning. She knew how important they were. She'd read the *Newsweek* article: **Dynamic duo transforms the advertising business in Los Angeles!** Her boys were in a magazine. They were the shit. When they bickered it humanized them. For Mila, it was like going backstage.

"Hi very fine," flirted Mila, punning Barry's name. He was hardly her type (too small and too funky), but Mila played him anyway. "Break any hearts this weekend?"

"Hell yes, sweetheart! I had to mow the lawn, right, so I took off my shirt to catch some rays. I'm telling you the desperate housewives went crazy." Barry struck a few model-like poses.

Mila giggled. "The hunk of Hancock Park! Yummy."

Vernon interrupted. "I'll have you know I'm serious about this parking memo."

Barry sighed, exasperated. "We have to park where we park, Vern. The disabled children's academy uses the lower level. You know that."

"They're not *all* disabled."

"You're going to burn for that, Vernon," interjected Mila.

"Ha! Like you never make fun of them."

"How can you say that – about me or them?"

"Come on, Mila. The chubby one. The kid with the cape."

"Humanology teaches us not to belittle those less fortunate than we are."

"Excuse me," replied Vernon, "but I think Christianity copyrighted that idea like two thousand years before your cult did."

"Humanology is not a cult. It's a legitimate religion."

"It's legitimately fucked up is what it is."

"So, are we meeting the folks from Dogwalkers.com today?" Barry asked, effectively shutting down their argument. New business was the ultimate trump card. It was the lifeblood of the agency. Mila knew this as well as Vernon.

Vernon sparked. "This afternoon with them, right Mila?"

"Nope, Thursday. Today is Buyalot.com"

"You mean Buymorestuff.com," corrected Barry.

"Out of business," said Vernon. "Buyalot bought them out."

Then Mila remembered. "Can either of you meet the VP of marketing for the Happy Soul Industry? His name is David Angelo. He called this morning to set up a time."

"Happy Soul Industry? What are they, a pharmaceutical?" Vernon laughed at his own joke. He didn't have to be in the creative department to be funny.

"Great name," mulled Barry. "I bet we could do some fabulous work with that."

Vernon was skeptical. "Yes, but what exactly is *that*."

"You know, I never asked," Mila answered. "But they must be doing something right. He's staying at the Four Seasons."

THREE

ONTRARY to Mila's comment about the weather, David Angelo had indeed gone for a swim in the Four Seasons pool. While living, he hadn't been much of a swimmer. Pools were scarce in the 1900s as was clean water. Manhattan's waterfront had mostly terrified him. Now the opposite held true. David zipped from one corner to the other like a speeding porpoise. That fast. That clean. He had to remind himself to come up for air in the off chance someone was watching. But at this late hour, and given the chill, what few people who were around had toweled off and left, leaving him to frolic uninhibited. And David took advantage. He didn't just walk on water he danced on top it! The angel knew he shouldn't make light of God's miracles but he couldn't help himself. While he possessed supernatural abilities, it was as if he'd regained aspects of his humanity as well: Exuberance. Playfulness. Perhaps even disobedience. For whatever reasons, the sheer pleasure of physical activity overwhelmed him, captivating his senses. Heaven was a cerebral place. To be there was joyous beyond all earthbound comprehension, yes, but it was very rarely fun. *This was fun.* There were no swimming pools in Heaven.

David twisted through the water, effortlessly turning over and moving forward. In his excitement, he never saw the lady swimming in front of him. He'd plunged into her abdomen like a torpedo.

Blindsided, she sank like an anchor.

Panic. He hadn't felt it in an age. Possessing no divine "cure" for drowning, he had to save this woman the old-fashioned way. Which meant getting her out of the water fast. He swam beneath her, grabbing her by the midriff. Plenty strong, he moved her body easily. David leapt out of the pool, risking being seen, nearly careening with a deck chair. He pushed it out of the way, spreading her body on the hard concrete. Even blue, she was obviously stunning, possessing an exquisite physique. Unfortunately, that lovely physique wasn't breathing. Moving the long black hair from the woman's face, David opened her mouth with one hand feeling for her tongue with the other. It wasn't there! She must've swallowed it at impact. The good news was that it might have inadvertently blocked a whole lot of water from entering her lungs.

An angel's fingers were very nimble, and David was able to quickly and efficiently negotiate the woman's curled tongue. Grasping it between his thumb and forefinger he gently pulled her tongue forward. Water rushed out behind it.

Firmly gripping her jaw he lowered his face over hers to perform artificial respiration, a modern skill he had no way of knowing. But yet it came to him like reflex. Was he being guided by a higher power? He put his mouth upon hers and blew. And it worked! The woman gasped, expectorating water. She sat up, leaned on a nearby chaise. Unable to speak, her breaths came rapidly.

David whispered a prayer of gratitude as well as an apology. "Thank you for not taking this vibrant life, dear Lord. Forgive me for having put it in jeopardy in the first place." He could only imagine the consequences if she had died, for him as well as for her. Would they both go to Heaven? And if so, would they cross paths? What would he say to her? People who arrived in Heaven early (because of unnatural death) were often unhappy to be there. And who could blame them? Heaven was never intended to be *better* than earth, merely after it. Such were the mysteries of life and after life.

Regaining consciousness, the woman's beauty only intensified. Her flesh acquired a luminous honey color. Mediterranean perhaps? Her eyes opened. She looked right at David causing him to blush, yet another emotive behavior he hadn't experienced in ages. David may have been an angel but he used to be a man.

She licked her lips, finally speaking: "Thank you," she whispered, "for saving my life."

He wondered: Did she know it was he who had almost ended it? Likely not. Very few individuals remembered their time prior to dying. The so-called "white light" was basically a euphemism for "I don't remember." A snow screen. David died suffering an aneurysm. He recalled having a really bad day and then a headache. And that was it.

"I don't know what happened. Normally, I'm an excellent swimmer." She considered standing. Waves of nausea rippled through her and she stayed put.

David confessed. "I'm afraid I collided with you in the pool. I was doing laps. My eyes were closed. The impact must've rendered you unconscious. I'm grateful to have been able to help." Despite regaining humanistic characteristics, he wasn't about to start lying. He'd alter the truth to save another person's life but not to a person whose life he'd just saved. Lying to avoid judgment was wrong, period. If rules existed for conducting oneself on Earth, God was pretty clear about that one.

"My name is Evelyn," she said, followed by, of all things, a hiccup. "Excuse me." And then she hiccupped again. "God, I'm sorry!"

"My name is David and don't you dare apologize to me." David positioned himself behind her. Without asking, he began patting her back. "My mother did this for me whenever I got the hiccups." Again, he blushed. Had he been this bold as a person? Granted, in his day no one had been that bold. But Evelyn yielded to him. She hiccupped a few more times, managing a laugh.

"It's working," she exhorted. "I think they're gone." She turned around and David's palm nearly caught her in the face. "Yikes!" But she was smiling.

"Well *that* would have taken the cake. Hitting you after nearly drowning you! I don't know what my problem is. Anyway, you must be freezing. Let me get you a towel." David jumped up, dashing over to the cabana desk. At first puzzled by the lack of staff, the angel recognized his good fortune in not being seen. His poolside acrobatics had defied explanation. David rushed the towel back to Evelyn.

"Thank you," Evelyn said. "My, I sure have been saying that a lot." She patted her face and arms before wrapping the towel around her waist. David noticed a small tattoo on her right hip: a black bird with piercing red eyes. He'd never seen markings on a lady. Only on boxers and sailors! Yet on Evelyn it was elegant as well as sexy. David bit his lower lip. Was he attracted to this woman? He hadn't thought about such things forever. The last lady he'd been with was his wife. And she'd died in 1927, ten years before him. After her death David did not take another spouse or even enter into a relationship. By then he'd become too old and, besides, those were decidedly more chaste times. The angel flashed for a moment on God's feminine presence but shook the thought away. She was a different matter. God did not inspire...*lust*.

"Listen David," Evelyn purred. "May I be forward? I want to do something for you, my way of expressing gratitude. Dinner this evening?"

"Evelyn-"

"If you say no I'm jumping back in the pool."

"Okay, okay, you win! Dinner would be swell. Only I can't do it tonight, Evelyn. What I mean to say is I've got a busy morning tomorrow and with all the excitement..." Butterflies alighted in his stomach exiting his throat. Angels didn't make dinner dates with mortals, especially if that mortal was a leggy bombshell with a tattoo on her hip. But it wasn't like angels searched for ad agencies either. Things were definitely askew. But David was resolute. He'd go out with this bombshell just as sure as he'd find God an advertising agency. He made a mental note to himself: Do not say "swell" in this woman's presence again.

"You're right, of course," Evelyn replied. "I probably should take it easy."

"How about tomorrow night?"

"It's a date! I'll make all the arrangements and pick you up here at eight." She beamed. "Mr. Angelo, I'm ever so happy to have *bumped* into you this afternoon."

David laughed at her joke. "Me too," he smiled. "But my surname. How did you know it?"

Evelyn was momentarily flustered. "Silly man. You told me before you pressed your mouth into mine. Always the gentleman."

"Funny, I don't recall-"

"Let me remind you then, Mr. Angelo." Evelyn wrapped her arms around David's neck giving him a delicate but lingering kiss.

The kiss hit David as hard as he'd hit her! He swooned.

"Tomorrow at eight?" she confirmed.

David nodded dumbly.

Evelyn then stripped the wet towel from her body, handed it to him, turned, and walked slowly away, aware of his eyes on her back.

David drew a bead on her provocative tattoo. The bird's piercing eyes met his. He felt something run up his spine, like a spider. Nerves? He shuddered, trying to shake the feeling.

From the hotel courtyard behind him came the tinkling of glasses and conversation. Turning orange, the sun had begun its descent. People were collecting in the garden for cocktails and dinner.

Angels don't dream because they don't really sleep. They drift. And as David Angelo drifted he saw Evelyn beckoning to him from illicit shadows beyond Heaven. He thrashed in bed trying to get to her.

FOUR

STEPPING out of his chauffeur-driven car, David marveled at this spectacle of modern architecture. Chloe, Night & Wiener was housed in a complex designed to resemble a prototypical television set from TV's golden age. The windows were structured as one big panel, mimicking a screen. Satellite dishes mounted the roof resembling rabbit ears. The main entrance was rounded like a knob. It was an effective ruse. Most of the comments had been complimentary. But because of its idiosyncratic design, many of the employees had windowless offices. The views belonged to management, which was where David Angelo was heading.

David struggled to find the elevator button on the smooth and slippery surface. Various colorful poles jutted from floor to ceiling. Was that how people got around these days? David was baffled.

Finally a meticulous Asian woman entered the lobby. She was

dressed completely in black, her belt and glasses matching leopard. "Mr. Angelo?" she queried, looking right at him.

"Correct!" responded David enthusiastically. "Thank you for rescuing me."

"A lot of people have trouble finding the button," she said to him. "It's just below the surface." She navigated the tricky wall, finding the nearly invisible button. When she pressed it the elevator spoke: Going up! Prepare to be moved!

David jumped.

Misreading his bewilderment, the greeter slipped into tour guide mode. "Television was one of the most important inventions of the twentieth century, Mr. Angelo. Our building captures that idea. Unfortunately, we may have to change it to a computer. Ha! Anyway, my name is Amy Su. I am Client Liaison."

The elevator doors opened revealing a translucent green, egg-like chamber. Amy continued her monologue. "The egg represents creativity. The birth of an idea."

"I must say, this is all very impressive," said David, admiring the futuristic elevator as it began its ascent. Heaven had colors like these but not the polymer.

The doors opened, and they were staring into the imposing grille of a shiny and black sport utility vehicle parked on the carpeted floor.

"My word, it's a car!" David exclaimed.

"The Path Maker XL. One of our client's most popular vehicles."

David paused to read the caption. "This land is your land, in the Path Maker XL."

"Right this way, Mr. Angelo. Vernon and Barry are very excited to meet you."

No last names, thought David. Interesting. "And what about Mr. Wiener?"

Amy stopped abruptly, pursing her lips. Apparently, she wanted him to lean closer. "We pronounce it 'winner.' Dick Wiener is the founder of this agency. But I'm afraid he's a bit reclusive."

They resumed walking. Framed advertisements adorned the walls on both sides of the hall. One of the agency's creations, the Taco-Laco

Dog, was featured prominently. Hanging from every available corner, monitors played a tape-loop of agency commercials. The place was a beehive, with hipsters buzzing in and out of their egg-shaped cubicles. The ambiance was intoxicating. David kept turning this way and that. The duo arrived at the Executive Corner, where Mila greeted them.

"Good morning, Mr. Angelo. Welcome to Chloe, Night & Wiener." At least one-quarter Puerto-Rican, Mila took pride in her vibrant heritage as well as her vivacious looks. That being said, she downplayed it whenever new business was lurking. Humanology taught her how and when to put the best foot forward. Instead of her usual tight-fitting MTV-inspired wardrobe, today she was a study in muted grays. Only her daring pumps pointed to Mila's livelier self.

Unsure how to properly greet this woman (and sensitive from his encounter with Evelyn) David gave Mila's hand a tentative squeeze. Even if not in style, at least being a gentleman was always appreciated. "Pleased to make your acquaintance," he said. "And by the way, thank you too, Amy!"

Amy smiled, bowed, and remained.

"Please take a seat," continued Mila. "It won't be long. Meantime can I get you anything – a Starbucks? Seattle's Best?"

"I'd prefer coffee, thank you." David took a seat. Or rather fell into one. The sofa was basically a malleable, large, beige ball of leather. It was *kind* of pretty and *sort* of comfortable. David regarded it and the rest of what he'd experienced so far with bemused affection. So this was what passed for "hip" these days. He browsed a magazine from the brushed metal table beside him. *Adweek* featured a doctored photograph of CN&W's Taco-Laco dog on the cover. The animal was holding what looked like a silver shoe in its mouth. The caption: **EVERY DOG HAS ITS DAY**... Below it, in smaller type the subhead: **Not to mention its Vernon Night!** David eagerly turned pages to find the story. Nothing wrong, he thought, with doing a little 11th-hour research.

And there she was, looking fantastic in a strapless black evening gown: Evelyn! In the photo she was shaking hands with the Mayor of New York City. Stunned, David read the caption aloud:

"T&R Chief Planning Officer, Ms. Evelyn Warren, expresses delight at the celebration of their new office space in the world famous Empire State Building. 'First King Kong and now T&R,' Ms. Warren said to the hundreds in attendance."

Before David could digest the news, Vernon Night greeted him. Wearing one of his trademark Armani suits, with only a ribbed black tee shirt under its jacket, Vernon was the embodiment of business casual, L.A. style. He extended a hand to David. Then laughed. "More to help you get out of that thing than for shaking." He pulled David up, before leading him into his office, where Barry was waiting. Amy trailed after them with coffee.

Vernon winked. "My partner, Barry Fine. He's our Chief Creative Officer. Some days he's even pretty good at it."

"Mr. Fine is a genius," Amy added. She placed the tray on a corner of Vernon's desk, bowing again. Barry pulled out his wallet, offering Amy a twenty. She ignored the glib gesture, preferring to continue her welcoming. "Mr. Angelo, we sincerely hope you make Chloe Night your new home."

"Thank you, Amy, for...*that*." Vernon said dryly.

Everyone sat as Amy exited, finally.

"Well, I happen to agree with her assessment of your work," David said to Barry. "Especially what you've done for Arrowhead Bikes. Your copy is brilliant." He'd done his homework on Chloe Night and wanted them to know it.

Flattered, Barry offered the twenty to David. "Here. You take it."

Vernon sighed. "Less about us for a moment...In lieu of presenting credentials we thought we'd frame this meeting as more of a learning session."

"Especially given we know almost nothing about you!" added Barry. "Did you know you're Google-proof?"

"Google proof. That's me." David had no idea what Barry meant. Perhaps it was a term used in the creative department.

"Yes, well," Vernon spoke up, "tell us Mr. Angelo, just what is the Happy Soul Industry? A start-up?"

David chuckled. He understood that term, even expected the

question. "I can assure you, gentlemen, we are not a start-up. Our organization has been working behind the scenes for some time." Having rehearsed with God, David spoke from memory. "We are more a service enabler than a maker of products. We represent goodness in all of its forms. Be it love, kindness, sharing, whatever. Maintaining this ubiquity is paramount to us. As you might imagine, we are affiliated with many known religions, past and present. We-"

Vernon had to interrupt. "Um, Mr. Angelo-"

"David."

"David. Before going any further you should know we aren't taking any more assignments pro-bono. I'm for goodness as much as the next guy but, well..."

"Jesus, Vernon," cried Barry. "Let the man complete a sentence."

David laughed. "Mr. Night, we have money. I can assure you of that. Our benefactors have very deep pockets. You will receive top dollar for your efforts." Here he paused for effect. "That is provided you are selected."

Self-consciously, Vernon stared at his pricey loafers. He'd mistaken the client for a penniless do-gooder.

"Nice going, Scrooge!" Barry had tried for funny but the remark had more bite.

"Don't feel bad, Mr. Night," said David. "It happens all the time. The image of goodness is mired by antiquated belief systems. People perceive those who are good as weak. Charity cases. And that's the crux of our problem. Perceived this way, the religions of the world aren't reaching the young and the ambitious. Frankly, we're not even getting close." He took a deep breath, albeit a fake one. The room was definitely listening to him now. "Goodness, or the pursuit of goodness, requires a massive overhauling of its brand image. We need to be relevant and contemporary. God is not a white-robed old man with silver mane. And he doesn't have to be. The Happy Soul Industry was set up to change all that. And not just about God. We want people to feel good about being good! We want an advertising campaign that encourages good acts from a society that is bereft of good acts. So in a sense the client is goodness, pure and simple."

Silence. They could hear the inane whelps of the Taco-Laco dog projecting from the televisions in the hall.

"Wow," Barry said. "There's a brief."

"Indeed," said David. "It may be the most important assignment in the world. Souls are at stake!"

Vernon cleared his throat. "Um, David, what exactly do you want the consumer to do – if consumer is even the right word?"

"The obvious. Go to church. More importantly, *like* going to church. Help those in need. Stop littering. Think before speaking poorly of others. Stop hurting one another. Get off drugs. Just be nicer in general. Have faith in God." He thought about his answer. Then added: "How do we get people to start certain behaviors while stopping others? You tell us."

"Us?" Vernon questioned. "Is there a management team?"

"I report to one…individual."

"So, this is a pitch then?" asked Barry. "You're talking to other agencies as well?" He'd figured as much. Clients never awarded their accounts without a review. Even the "nice" ones.

"Per my boss's counsel I'm doing the diligence. Rest assured, gentlemen, win or lose, you will be paid for your speculative work."

Vernon's relief was palpable. "I see," he said. Looking at his partner, he continued: "I'm sure we have questions. Lots of them. But I think we could use a bit of time to sort things out."

"Of course," replied David. He removed an envelope from inside his jacket and handed it to Vernon. "Here is your brief, in writing. If you have additional questions, I can be reached at the hotel." The angel stood up, sensing the meeting was coming to a close.

Vernon and Barry followed suit. They all shook hands. "We'll be in touch, David. And soon," Vernon exhorted.

Barry added: "Do you need validation?"

"Of course not!" David answered. "I know you. You know me. That's all the validation I need."

"I think he means for parking," said Vernon, trying not to sound condescending.

"Parking? I don't even know how to drive!"

"Funny. Neither does Vernon." Barry could not resist making that joke, even more poignant given Vernon's madness in the garage.

Ignoring his partner, Vernon opened the doors. "Mila, will you please show our guest to the elevator?"

Taking David by the elbow she escorted him out. They were again surrounded by the sounds and visuals of people working and the agency's reel playing from above.

As soon as they were out of earshot, Vernon turned to his partner. "What just happened here?"

"I have an uncle who doesn't know how to drive either. But he's blind so that's not really the same thing."

"Enough with the jokes. Do you think Angelo's legit? I mean we can't even find his company on line."

"Who cares, if he pays his bills?"

"*If.*"

"Hey, he said he'd pay us for spec. How many clients do that?"

"Yeah, well, what if he pays us in magic fairy dust? I mean goodness in all its forms. What the hell is that?"

"Hold on, Vern. If he is on the level, from a creative perspective it's a great assignment. We'll win millions of awards and look like saints in the process."

Vernon considered the point, warming to the idea. "A chauffeur. The Four Seasons. They gotta have bucks."

Mila knocked on the door, entering. She never waited for an invite. "Odd bird. Nice guy though."

"Did he speak to you?" Vernon asked.

"All men speak to me."

"Seriously," said Barry, "what did he say?"

"He asked me if I knew a nice place to buy clothes."

"Oh Lord," sniped Vernon. "Where did you send him – The Merry Go Round?"

"Screw you, Vernon."

"I knew it!" Barry shouted. "He must be suiting up for the other agency." Now he was more determined than ever. "I say we go for it."

"What the hell! I could use a little goodness in my life."

"You think?" Mila asked.

FIVE

EING an angel, David didn't have to shave, shower or do much of anything in the way of grooming and self-maintenance. If he consumed food and drink then he would defecate and pass water. If he did not then he wouldn't. His beard remained one length, not even his nails grew. Actually, it was a pretty sweet deal. He maintained his physique without effort. It was the same for all emissaries of Heaven. An angel's body functioned bodily only when called upon.

Still, David prepared. He had a date tonight, the first one in over a hundred years! Understandably, he was nervous. And grooming pacified him. But was his anxiety more serious than that? Could his "date" tonight be crossing a line? Worse yet, was he betraying God?

Ancient was the controversial relationship between sex and religion. Even an angel could get confused. Sin was an awfully big word, potent with shadowy meaning. It was also something David hadn't discussed with God, ever.

Dripping wet, having just emerged from the shower, David stared at his naked body in the bathroom mirror. He couldn't help but look down at his penis. It had been a long time since he contemplated that part of his body. When he returned to the mirror, the Lord was staring back. "My God!" David reached for a towel, covering himself.

"It's okay, David. I've seen one before. Besides, I know why you're nervous. You're on Earth now. A man. Your vital parts are vital again."

"I'm sorry for startling. I meant no disrespect. But it's hard being naked in front of you."

Laughing sweetly, God reached through the mirror, picking up a tiny scented bar of soap. She smelled it. "I adore jasmine. You know, I created jasmine especially for the human body. For people to appreciate."

David remained quiet. He was embarrassed. He continued to adjust the towel, struggling to forge a knot.

God, of course, felt his worry. "Already self-conscious? How quickly we regain our human fears. People assume God is a prude, don't they?" She placed the soap back into its dish. "But sensuality is among my greatest gifts. Making love is meant to be divine. That's why it is a precursor to creation."

"I take it you know about my date?"

God wrinkled her eyes at him.

"Of course you know. Being God and all. I'm sorry. Nerves."

"Nervous is good, David. Not a frailty. It means you care. It means you worry about doing something wrong...or right. I wish more people were nervous."

"I can't imagine you ever being nervous," David said, respectfully.

"You should have seen me at Creation. I was a wreck." God reached out through the mirror, taking David's hand. "Come with me!"

"Where my Lord?"

"To the Garden!" God exclaimed, pulling him into the glass.

Renowned in countless paintings, etchings, and murals: The Garden of Eden. From every vantage point a perfect landscape. God and David happened upon a small clearing, surrounded by nature's greatest hits. Verdant hills blossomed upward to the north. A majestic waterfall roiled behind them. Limpid pools formed by their feet. Idyllic.

"This, David, is where it all began," said God, wistfully.

"I'm speechless." He approached a flowering bush to admire its blooms. The petals shimmered like butterfly wings. And the butterflies glimmered like flowers! "It's paradise."

"That was the idea. But when I submitted it to the Creative Review Committee it was met with a fair amount of criticism. The mountains were too high. The river was crooked. One committee member even found my chirping birds annoying."

David was incredulous. "You had to submit the Garden of Eden to a committee for approval? But you're God!"

"I am *a* God. The universe is a big place. Titles lose their meaning." With a wave of her hand a chorus of cerulean birds alighted from their perch in the trees. Birds of Paradise, no less! "Worse than the criticism, they had me work in the idea of Original Sin. As if my concept needed more drama."

"Did you have to obey this committee?"

God sighed. "I'm sure they would have killed Creation if I hadn't. Can you imagine? I was too close to production to give it all up. My ego would not allow that." She ambled to the water's edge and peered in. Her reflection rippled back. David followed. "My compromises are why the world has so many problems." God spoke softly, distracted by her own thoughts.

David had never seen her like this before. He wondered if anybody had, angel or mortal. "Don't judge yourself harshly."

God had to laugh. "If I don't who will?"

"Your creation is perfect. If the world were anything like this we wouldn't need an advertising campaign."

"That was the plan! But times change." God placed a finger in the water, creating ripples. David gazed upon them, observing his reflection in the moving water.

ONCE AGAIN, HE faced himself in the mirror. Unclenching his fist, he opened it slowly, revealing the beautiful flower from Heaven. He set it down gingerly, next to the jasmine bar.

David felt a rush of excitement about the coming evening. God hadn't bristled about the notion of him dating. She'd barely mentioned it. If God was all right with something then it was all right! She'd just taken him to the Garden of Eden. It's not like She was holding back.

But it was growing late and he had to hurry. David put on a shirt, buttoning it quickly. Then the tie. He twisted it this way and that. But he couldn't fathom how to tie it. What's the problem?

Then he remembered his wife. "Jenny! You always put on my tie." It had been one of their little rituals, one of those things a couple did that distinguished them as a couple.

From a simple chain worn around his neck, David removed and opened a small locket. Few personal articles made the trip to Heaven. This one, however, had never left his body. Inside was Jenny's photograph.

"My beloved, what am I doing?" David hadn't seen his wife since that rainy afternoon in the hospital. In the afterlife, in God's presence, he seldom missed her. But in the darkening hotel room, David was suddenly bereft.

He shut the locket. Then he removed his tie. "Nobody wears them in this town anyway."

Of the two suits he bought, he chose the olive colored one. Perhaps in some way it was an olive branch extended to his wife. Maybe, too, by not wearing a tie he was respecting their marriage as well.

He regarded himself in the mirror. Funny, he realized, mirrors didn't exist in Heaven. Appearances meant far more to the living, didn't they? Even though so much of life was blurry, people wanted to see themselves clearly. Yes, it was vanity. But on a deeper level, mirrors helped bring things into focus, reminding people that they occupied space in God's creation – that they existed at all.

SIX

HE hotel's aptly titled Seasons Bar was a serious watering hole for heavy hitters from the television and film industry. If only David knew what the stars of this generation looked like. He searched the room, surreptitiously glancing over the rim of a surprisingly pleasant pinot noir. The place was busy and he saw a lot of people who certainly looked like celebrities. People were preternaturally handsome, very fit, sun-tanned.

What he didn't know was how many advertising professionals from around the world congregated here. L.A. was where the vast majority of TV commercials were produced and the Four Seasons was where many of their producers stayed. Despite being the stepchild of Show Business, the two professions had a lot in common. Instead of two-hour films, thirty seconds. Instead of the Academy Awards, the Silver Slipper.

Behind David a boisterous group from New York were getting in their cups. Loud and obnoxious, they brayed about clients and each other with reckless abandon. David cringed. Thank God New Yorkers lost that hideous accent upon arriving in Heaven. He wondered why God had given it to them in the first place.

On and on they went ripping on other people's careers and reputations, in diatribes the Devil would appreciate.

As an aggregate, they embodied – for David, anyway – much of what was wrong about the world. Bad enough to have callous disregard toward other men. But to one's friends? David had forgotten how vile human behavior could get.

He tried to recall how it had been at the insurance agency. His memories were vague, as Heaven cleaned one's mind of such detritus. But he couldn't imagine it had been like this...like them.

He savored his wine. It was unlikely that an advertising campaign, no matter how deft, could change the likes of them. More unlikely, David reasoned, could such a crew come up with an ad campaign that might!

A Junior Account Executive from their ranks spilled one of the five Scotches he was carrying back to the table on David's shoe. Instead of apologizing, the young man made an observation: "Hey, Bro, that's single malt. You know what one of those cost me?"

"Good thing it's your client's money, eh sport?" Evelyn said, sidling between them. "Otherwise, you'd miss your student loan payment." Evelyn's comment, as well as her outright beauty, basically shut the kid down. He retreated to his table. "Junior AE's are the worst. They act so entitled." She gave David a kiss on the cheek.

"Evelyn, you certainly know how to make an entrance!"

Indeed, Evelyn could have walked out of an ad. Her jet-black hair cascaded over her silk blouse like a prop. She had on vintage diamond earrings and a pair of antique, wire-rimmed glasses, making her look both brilliant and sexy. And as far as David was concerned, she was.

"Please sit down," said David. An empty chair presented itself.

"I made a reservation at the Ivy," Evelyn said. "I hope that's not too obvious."

"I'm sure the Ivy is wonderful." David had no idea. "Can I get you a drink or is the atmosphere here too raucous?" He gestured toward the loud table. Even now he caught several of the men gaping at Evelyn.

"A drink would be divine. And don't worry about *them*. They're harmless. Unless you consider the work they do!"

Laughing, David signaled the bartender, ordered. "Do you know them?" he asked, surprised and maybe concerned.

"The way they're carrying on, everyone in this hotel knows them. But yes, we're in the same business." She fished a pistachio out of the nut tray. "I apologize on behalf of the American Association of Advertising Agencies."

So far so good, mulled David. If Evelyn had an ulterior motive for going out with him she wasn't acting that way. He didn't feel played. But he had to ask another question: "Evelyn, what about me? Do you know who I am?"

"Sure, you're the cute man who saved my life. And you're not wearing a wedding ring."

Flustered, David instinctively felt his barren ring finger.

"You're not married are you?"

"I...I was. She passed away."

"I'm sorry." Evelyn paused, placing her hand on his. "Listen, David, I need to tell you something about me as well. We have something in common. I run the planning department at Town & Robertson in New York."

Relieved by her admission, David nearly gasped. "I know! I saw your picture in a magazine."

"The *Adweek* piece? I'm not sure I liked that photograph."

"Nonsense," blurted David. "It's beautiful."

From the bar's corner the pianist began his set, launching into an old standard. Evelyn leaned closer to David. "So, Mr. Angelo. Tell me about yourself."

"It's a long story."

"Give me the headlines now. You can tell me the rest at dinner."

"Okay. But don't laugh." David pondered how best to answer. He opted for the facts, such as they were. "I work for an organization that represents goodness. Goodness in all its forms."

"Do you? Shame. I was hoping we could be a little bad tonight."

Blushing, David continued. "Actually, I'm looking for an advertising agency to help market the company."

"I've got news for you, David. I'm not so sure the world is interested in goodness in all its forms. It's badness people want. It's badness that sells."

"Lord knows it will be challenging," he said to Evelyn. *Badness sells.* A disturbing notion to say the least.

Suddenly, David felt cramped. "I could use some air before dinner. Do you mind if we go for a walk?"

"The Ivy is close by. Why don't we just walk there? I'll have the car sent over."

Evelyn made a sad face. "Are you going to be okay?"

David came back with a smile. "I'll be fine. Just hungry is all."

SEVEN

VERNON stood before the picture window in his office overlooking Los Angeles. The sky outside was a bluish purple preparing for night. His eyes glossed over the familiar panorama. The same few tall palm trees blew this way and that against the Santa Ana winds. In silhouette, they resembled the trees Vernon drew as a boy with a magic marker: A black line with seven or eight smaller ones exploding from the tip. He'd paint the coconuts last, just circles under the lines.

Vernon picked up one of his numerous award statues from the cabinet beneath the window. It wasn't his coveted Slippy but rather a humanitarian prize the agency won doing a campaign for the YMCA. The mayor had made a big deal of the project, honoring CN&W at an enormous party thrown at the tony Santa Monica Airport. The following day two favorable stories ran in the papers. The commercials would later garner the agency a slew of industry awards for creative achievement, including the one in his hand.

Of course, Vernon couldn't have cared less about the YMCA of Santa Monica. They'd done the pro-bono to appease the city (their snazzy new office required many hard-to-get permits) and they did the work to win awards.

Mission accomplished. Twice.

Once upon a long time ago, Vernon may have wondered if the agency's self-serving policies were ethical. Not anymore. Hell, even Barry – a big liberal – looked at pro-bono as merely a mine for awards. For a creative boutique like theirs, winning accolades meant almost as much as selling a client's product.

Vernon dropped the statue, upsetting the others, breaking some. Bric-a-brac rolled and fell onto the floor, joining the fallen portrait of his wife, its glass already cracked. Unfazed, Vernon left the mess.

For in his other hand Vernon held a sizable tumbler of Scotch, of which he now took a sip. Then another. He regarded the debris below: a slew of broken awards and a busted marriage.

Three loud raps interrupted his reverie. Keys jangling, the nightly cleaning lady entered his office. She seemed surprised to see the important executive standing in the gloaming, alone. "I'm so sorry. Am I disturbing you? I can come back."

"No, not at all." Vernon replied. "Come on in. It's kind of dirty in here."

The cleaning lady smirked, and headed toward him. As she approached, Vernon got a better look at her. And it was an eyeful. Her outfit was more French maid than union local. In addition, she was very made up for the late shift. Her lipstick shined. "So, where do you want me to start working?"

"Well," Vernon swallowed, "I know my knob could use polishing."

"You're the boss, honey." Dropping her props (a mop and bucket), the prostitute knelt down before him. Slowly, she began loosening Vernon's belt.

Vernon held up his drink, offering a toast to no one in particular. "Here's to goodness in all its forms," he said. "Oh, yeah."

EIGHT

ROMOTE goodness to the American people. That was his mission. And to think, Barry wasn't even a Republican. He contemplated initial concepts. He preferred to attack a new assignment by himself. Later he'd expose the ideas to his creative partner, Irma. Then Vernon.

Unlike Vernon's opulent, presidential office, Barry's domain had the aura of a war room, which in fact is what he called it during the concept phase of a project. Art and copy were everywhere, on the walls, on the rounded table in the center, scattered about the floor. Everywhere.

He lacked an official brief, having only the contents of the envelope they'd gotten from David. Which was fine. Barry liked things simple and unfettered. The less process in the creative process the better.

That's where a lot of other ad agencies screwed up. They liked to throw an army at every problem, even a non-problem, and especially where new business was concerned.

Unfortunately, these armies usually contained two or more bickering generals. Things could get strained and often did. Egos clashed. Pitches got bungled. Titled men often regarded themselves as renegade knights, each one wanting to save the princess. They may have started out with likeminded allegiances but it was only a matter of time before a knight reached for his sword. The moral: Just because an agency had resources didn't mean it had to use them.

Brilliant ideas seldom originated via committee. Yet committees had a way of popping up, like mushrooms. Whenever management intervened, the advertising became political and usually worse. Barry supposed Vernon would assign an account person to Happy Soul. He may have already. But a great idea could predicate next steps and he wanted to find it before a process was implemented. It was an ego thing and he admitted it.

Creator of the Marlboro Man, the Pillsbury Doughboy, and countless other advertising icons, even legendary ad man Leo Burnett extolled the virtues of what he'd called "the lonely man." The lonely man rolled up his sleeves and stayed late. Did whatever it took to get the job done. Armed with only paper and pencil, it was He and the assignment.

Barry could relate. He was mad into it now, the office's mess accentuating his demeanor. He perspired, as if in a kitchen. Miles Davis played loudly.

He was cooking theme lines or tags, the nucleus of most advertising campaigns. A tag dictated what one heard or read or saw before it. A line could sum up the entire brand. *Nothing runs like a Deere. Just do it.* Marker in one hand, tape roll in the other, Barry paced before his work. He wrote: ON EARTH AS IT IS IN HEAVEN. He wrote: BE GOOD FOR GOODNESS SAKES. He wrote: BE NICE! Nothing clicked.

For inspiration, he'd hung artifacts on the wall, photographs and all manner of religious propaganda: Pictures of Jesus. Icons. Churches.

Spotting the famous Nike line Barry laughed, wrote: JUST DO UNTO OTHERS! He doodled a smiley face on the edge of his pad. He wished he had something like that. A symbol that was as universal and compelling as the once ubiquitous happy face or the "I ♥ NY" slogan from the 1970s.

One of the most admired copywriters in the country, a revered forward thinker, yet Barry still took inspiration from the popular culture of his youth. Retroactive imagery appealed to him. What moved people in the past might do so again. He pointed to Altoids' *curiously strong mints* campaign as a prime example. He called it "retro-chic" for its use of old circus and movie pictures.

Ironically, in a business built on buzz, Barry was old school. He still liked baseball cards and Ferris wheels. He worshiped his copy of *Obvious Adams* and quoted from his signed original of Alan Arkin's *The Lemming Condition.*

Unlike him, a lot of copywriters thought purely in terms of new. Ideas only had to be original to be good. Unfortunately for them (and their clients), being of the moment was more important than being on the money, timeliness valued more than timelessness.

Barry knew that being good was a timeless idea. But it had an aura of negativity: *Are you a good person? Have you been bad?* That part wasn't resonating anymore. That was the bit that felt old. Scaring people was wrong. One needn't visit the ghetto to justify buying a home in the suburbs. Likewise, one needn't show someone Hell when making a pitch for Heaven. Fire and brimstone may have worked once but now it played like a movie of the week.

What if the Happy Soul Industry treated goodness as an invitation, a welcome as opposed to an admonishment, something pointing to the benefit of being good, the experience? How would that go? *Mmmm, Mmmm. Good!*

But the Happy Soul Industry wasn't soup and it wasn't for sale, either. As far as Barry knew, a philanthropist had set up a company whose only agenda was getting people enamored with goodness.

But if HSI wasn't a brick and mortar operation, or a website, then what was it? An enigma was awfully hard to advertise!

Barry stared at his notes one last time. He knew he didn't have the big idea yet. Creative lightning was rare, most bolts fizzling quickly without any real thunder. A good copywriter was his own toughest critic and Barry killed his creations like a guppy swallowed her young.

Maybe he should take a cue from the liquor industry. After all, they sold happiness in a bottle. And satisfaction. And coolness. And just about every other desirable attribute people perceived they were lacking. He drew a picture of a bottle with a halo above it. ABSOLUT GOODNESS, he scribbled beneath the image.

With a sweep of his hand, Barry cleared off a portion of his writing table. From a small vial, he tapped out two white pills. Taking the blunt end of one of his Slippy awards he crushed the opiates into a powder. In two snorts, he inhaled them into his nostrils.

The jazz reached a crescendo as Barry fell into his chair.

He wasn't the first creative person who used drugs for inspiration. Nor would he be the first to become addicted. As Barry drifted into narcosis, he couldn't help but note the irony of using dope and working on the Happy Soul Industry.

NINE

DESPITE the chill they sat outside at Ivy. Evelyn's New York skin was thick, unfazed by the temperature. An angel, David felt neither the cold nor the heat lamps.

Evelyn finished her crab cakes, passable but not up to the hype. *What out here was?*

David ordered grouper, but he'd done more talking than eating, much of it about his big day at Chloe Night. To a rapt audience, he'd described the architecture, the people, and every detail.

Evelyn had read about the building and knew all too well its inhabitants. CN&W had been the flavor of the month for nearly two years. Evelyn would be remiss had she not clamored to know why. Until David, she'd never met anyone who'd been inside the place.

Evelyn craved some gossip she could hold against them! Chloe Night avoided planning, her skill-set. Evelyn had attended Vernon's infamous speech on the subject, where she'd heard him state that planning in the U.S. was "mostly for agencies trying to appear *with it.*" Agencies like T&R.

Pissed, but envious too, Chloe Night's iconoclastic persona was far sexier than her company's old-boy network. Perception meant a lot in the ad world. Evelyn wasn't the only agency executive losing sleep over these West Coast hot shots.

As soon as the busboy took their plates a waiter brandished dessert menus.

Evelyn did not require a menu. The Ivy made a killer crème brûlée. She pitched the treat to David as if it were the subject of an advertising campaign, rhapsodizing about its virtues. "It's positively sinful."

David had no choice but to comply.

Two tables down a television actor bickered with his agent but David and Evelyn paid scant attention. Their eyes were locked, the intensity between them growing.

The dessert arrived. She impaled the treat with a spoon, its glistening surface crackling under the pressure.

David had never seen a food item like this before. He broke through its hardened sugary top, smiling at the sheer joy of doing so. He rolled a spoonful of the delectable concoction around in his mouth, savoring the sweetness as it melted away.

Earth certainly had its pleasures and he wallowed in them now: A beautiful dinner companion. Dining al fresco. Crème brûlée. At that moment it became hard to fathom why he'd been sent here at all. Goodness was all around them. Why did people need a campaign to see it? He was glad to be alive. Wasn't everybody?

"May I ask you a personal question?"

"Aren't they all?" she replied.

"Do you believe in God?"

Evelyn placed her spoon beside the half-empty dish. "I believe in good and evil," she said.

"Which one do you think is more prevalent?" David stopped eating, intent on hearing her reply.

"Tonight? Or in general?" She licked her spoon, aiming for naughty.

He wanted to know her real answer. "In general."

Evelyn toyed with her food, pushing the remaining sugary shards from one side of the bowl to the other. This was a cigarette moment. But she had to refrain, as the maitre-d' loomed. "Where I come from there's a saying: 'You marry good but you sleep with evil.' I don't know, I think people are capable of both." She resumed eating.

Getting the impression she didn't want the conversation going deeper, David eased up. He took a cue from her previous comment. "Where are you from?" he asked. He'd been wondering for some time. She possessed an exotic look hard to pinpoint. Even surrounded by television and film stars, she stood out.

"The old country," she said, sipping water. They'd passed on coffee.

"Not the answer I expected," replied David. When he'd lived the old country meant Eastern Europe. He gazed at her, curiously.

Evelyn laughed. She'd seen this look of confusion before. "My passport states I was born in Jerusalem, but my roots are in the river basin of Egypt. You can imagine the trouble I have in airports."

The Middle East! David nearly gasped. The Nile basin was the cradle of civilization. Jerusalem one of God's first *locations.* And yet, by God's own admission, She had overplayed Her hand there. Tried to do too much. And too soon. The populace had become overloaded by stimuli, frustrated, and then horribly angry. Now Jews, Muslims, and Christians bickered relentlessly. It was God's worst heartache, Her biggest regret. The region she had chosen to represent goodness was now anything but. Arab nations and Israel were forever at each other's throats and Jerusalem was ground zero.

David held back his emotion. Not now, he thought. Not here. "I knew you were from somewhere special," he said.

Evelyn placed her hand upon his, barely touching it, yet David felt a charge like an electric current. His recollection was vivid:

He's on holiday in Michigan with his new wife. It's an unusually balmy evening and they're sitting on the beach beneath the lighthouse. Only married one year, this is their first trip together. She puts her hand on his and the lighthouse beacon shines on them, just like a camera flash, freezing the moment forever.

David's eyes glazed. He almost spoke her name: Jenny.

"You're thinking about the past," she said. "I can tell." She lifted his hand, looking at the palm. She scrutinized the lines crisscrossing its surface. "How old are you?" she asked.

The question caught David off guard. There was no way he could tell her the truth. Again he marveled how often lying became necessary cavorting among the living. "Thirty-eight," he said, choosing his age the year his wife died.

"You have an old soul," Evelyn responded, "but you seem so full of life. So virile."

David's heart leapt into his throat, thrilled but rife with anxiety. For all he knew he didn't look thirty-eight at all. Maybe he even appeared younger! Or perhaps the opposite held true and Evelyn was just being nice. Lost in all this, of course, was her reference to his soul.

"Well, I exercise some," replied David, lamely. In his entire life he'd never been this fit. For that he could thank God, literally. She'd made sure he looked good for his new position on Earth. "The advertising business is all about image," She'd said. "Whether I like it or not, your looks mean a lot. And so you will have yours." David wondered if he would even be on this date had his appearance been otherwise.

"We have to try," claimed Evelyn. Paranoia over one's age was rampant and being in a chic Beverly Hills eatery only exacerbated the situation. Evelyn knew full well how important it was to keep up appearances. Your perceived edge depended on it.

"Edge," just like in the movie business, was synonymous with youth. Older executives could sit down at the ad game's bigger tables (in emeritus, on boards, etc.) but they seldom got dealt any cards. If and when they did most of these journeymen bluffed.

It was easier to stay in the room by *not* participating. Play your cards right and there was always a chance you'd be kicked upstairs into a lucrative, if meaningless, position. At least then you'd get to keep your summer home.

As a result, a majority of agency elders spent their waning years trying not to be found out. Again, just as in Hollywood, experience meant very little. It was the antithesis of edge. Experience meant you'd been grazing too long. Unless your last name was on the door (and sometimes even then), having a long career meant you were long in the tooth.

"Let's get out of here." Evelyn caught the waiter's eye, an easy task for someone as good looking as she.

SHE CALLED IT a BMW, which he correctly remembered as the initials for Bavarian Motor Works, a firm that made some of the world's first aircraft engines. And judging from the roadster Evelyn was powering up Doheny Drive, they still did.

He gripped the leather seat beneath his fanny, blinking his eyes against the wind. Turning onto Sunset Boulevard, David was prompted to keep them open. The gaudy lights, billboards, storefronts, and the people: what strange breeds parading up this strip! Into The Rainbow Club, The Whiskey, The Chateau Marmot.

Overstimulated, David almost ducked when they passed under a massive billboard. But then he would have missed it: A group of angels cavorting around a woman barely clothed. She held a bottle of perfume like an apple. Art imitating life? It was all too much for the earthbound angel. And it was not over yet.

Evelyn turned left off the strip onto a dark and narrow street and proceeded up a surprisingly steep piece of road. Driveways were apparent but not the houses. Higher and higher they climbed, the car whining on the curves.

"Are we still in Hollywood?" David risked sounding ignorant. He was startled by the sudden change in terrain.

"This is where Hollywood roosts when it's not foraging for crumbs down below! We're almost there."

Evelyn assumed his question had been rhetorical. She worked the steering wheel this way and that, never letting up on the gas. That is until she hit the brakes, stopping abruptly.

She backed up a few yards, pulling into a graveled median, not very wide, edging an overlook.

And what an overlook! The city of Los Angeles glittered up at them like something otherworldly, a matrix of bright colors and tiny moving lights, like nothing David had ever seen, even in Heaven. When he'd been a boy L.A. was but a growing township between the desert and the Pacific. But this...

"Pretty, eh?" Evelyn commented, knowing she didn't have to.

"I bet they call L.A. the City of Angels because it looks like Heaven."

"That, or it's the baseball team." Evelyn winked.

Funny. On top of everything else, Evelyn was quick-witted.

David witnessed a line of planes silently drifting toward the airport and, briefly, had no idea what they were.

Was that sweat under his arms? Could she hear his heart beating?

Then she kissed him, not gently either, leaning into it like a movie star. They melted into one another, two figures in an expressionist canvas.

When Evelyn pulled away he tumbled toward her helplessly. It was as if she had a gravitational pull. He needed to be closer to her. He missed her lips already.

"Let's not start something we can't finish." She gave him the sweetest look but yet there was her hand coming up in between them.

David was mystified. "You started it," he mumbled. Granted, he'd come of age in an era when women ran hot and cold. But he hadn't expected this kind of fickleness from Evelyn. Of course he hadn't expected her to kiss him either. Not like *that.*

Aroused and confused, David leaned back, licked his lips, tasting her again. He would happily indulge this splendid creature. He had no choice. Evelyn's gravity had him in her orbit. Right now even God's pull felt slighter. He wasn't an angel anymore. He was with one.

"You're a very attractive man, David. And this is a very romantic place. A woman could..." She gave his thigh a little squeeze. "...*You know*."

He knew. David considered a more forceful approach. He had to have this woman. He'd do anything. "Let's change the subject," he said, with assertion. If only he could say something witty and seductive. If only he could have another kiss. "A proposition," he said.

"Oh," Evelyn replied. Provoked, she leaned toward him. "Pray tell, Mr. Angelo. What might that be?"

"How would you like to pitch the Happy Soul Industry account?" David beamed. The brazen question made him giddy. He wasn't thinking about God. He was thinking about a goddess. Shooting from the hip, literally and figuratively.

"Excuse me," Evelyn said. "Do you know what that sounds like?"

"Yep." David dismissed her suspicious tone. He half expected it. Earlier he'd felt that way about her!

Furrowing her brow, Evelyn touched his lip with her index finger. "And tell me, does your offer have anything to do with what just transpired between us?"

"Maybe," he said. "But who cares?"

David elaborated, growing more passionate as he spoke. "Evelyn, it's a good move. For both of us. CN&W is a great West Coast agency. Why not see how a bigger firm might handle the assignment? That way I get two viewpoints. And it means I'll see you again."

It was obvious how smitten he was. If this were proof then so be it. You only live twice. He sweetened the pie: "It would be your lead that brings the account. Your get. Not only are you the head of planning but you're bringing in business."

He sensed the wheels turning in her beautiful head. Evelyn Warren was in the highest tier of upper management. No way she was going to walk away from new business. He had her. He could tell.

"Would we even have a chance?" she asked, giggling at the prospect. "I mean, Chloe Night & Wiener..."

David knew he couldn't award her the account right here and now. "Look at it this way," he said. "You'd have someone in your corner."

He stopped talking when her tongue entered his mouth. It slipped between his teeth and he sucked on it gently. They both were getting what they wanted.

THEY'D MOVED TO David's hotel room but only because Evelyn's road-ster lacked a back seat. His body had indeed functioned, twice. Smok-ing a cigarette, Evelyn coiled beside David.

In darkness, he tracked the burning tip. It floated above her face like a firefly. Down to her mouth and swiftly back up. The smoke didn't bother him. Nothing Evelyn did bothered him. David couldn't believe his new life.

Silently, he thanked God again for sparing her life at the pool and now for letting him be a part of it. He touched Evelyn's smooth abdo-men with the back of his hand, letting a nail drag across the skin. He could feel her dimpling under his touch.

"Are you kidding?" Evelyn gasped. "That would make three times tonight!"

"But it's the first time this morning," purred David. He nuzzled closer to her, rubbing his nose against her warm stomach. His sexual prowess was supernatural, a gift from God. It had to be.

Evelyn laughed. "Can't you see I'm smoking?"

"You certainly are."

"Don't get me wrong. I think it's heavenly," she replied, recklessly tossing her cigarette out the window and over the terrace.

From below, the soft chatter and tinkling of a late-evening party drifted aimlessly upward like embers from a campfire, the sound all but gone by the time it reached their altitude. Maybe the cigarette landed in the pool. Maybe it was sitting on top of an expensive hair-cut.

Evelyn slid the covers down revealing the rest of her body.

David accepted the invitation with a discernible moan. He slid his mouth downward across her stomach, lightly depositing kisses, gently pinching her taut flesh with his teeth.

Stopping at her belly, he noticed her tattoo again, its red eyes glaring at him in the darkness. It was not a pretty creature. Actually, it was vaguely menacing…a very dirty bird, indeed.

David shut his eyes. He worked his way down Evelyn's torso. His carnal desire was overpowering.

Hard again, he opened her up with his tongue.

TEN

DOWNSTAIRS in the courtyard, amidst all the chatter and laughter, under the twinkling lanterns, beside the rippling waters of the Four Seasons' pool, an elegantly dressed woman – a guest of honor as it so happened – was contemplating suicide.

Just take the rest of my Valium, Erin Night thought, and jump into the goddamn pool. *Be done with it already*. Vernon won't give a shit and neither will anybody else at this party. Erin rolled her eyes at the cigarette butt that floated across the water. Advertising people were so classy.

She scanned the crowd and quickly found her husband. He was telling his golfing-with-the-gay-client story to a trio of blowsy, tipsy women. It wasn't that Erin could hear him, she could just *tell*. He always told the story and he always told it to women.

As usual, they indulged him, laughing uproariously. Erin feigned wonderment but she knew why women fawned over her estranged husband. He looked like a mid-career Jack Nicholson and acted the part. He had money. He was straight. And his soon-to-be ex-wife was a bitch.

His increasing indifference toward her she could take. That's what shopping and girlfriends were for. But autumn always begets winter, and when every last leaf had fallen from the proverbial tree, the chill in their marriage had simply become unbearable. Vernon had devolved into a cynical, distant, and mean human being. And, honestly, so had she. His philandering was merely a side effect. Why they were both still together (even if only on paper) was as mysterious as America's love affair with that insipid talking dog he helped create.

She looked up and saw Vernon gabbing with another grinning lady. In the midst of an overly fey golf swing, he was as predictable as their marriage was bad.

A thin, slightly stooping fellow approached her. She didn't recognize him at first. Phil Connors worked in the I.T. department at Chloe Night. Right now he was working on his third rum punch. Like a frat boy he drank it from a beer glass.

"Might you have a light tonight, Mrs. Night?" An unlit cigarette flailed around in his mouth. Laughing at his rhyme he lost his balance and almost fell into the pool.

Erin caught him, grabbing him by the elbow. "If anyone dies in the pool tonight, it's me."

Phil didn't know what she was talking about. "Guess what?" he asked, trying to compose himself. "Kato Kaelin is in the Jacuzzi. I saw him take his shirt off."

"And I see my husband talking to one of his former conquests," replied Erin blithely. "I'm sure the Jacuzzi is only a matter of time. Come to think of it, he and Kato would make a great team. O.J. all over again." She enjoyed telling on Vernon, even if in vain. It was the first enjoyable moment she'd experienced since coming to Chloe Night's tenth anniversary party. She'd been married that long and frankly the number had lost all its magic.

"Former conquest? That's Mila who's talking to your, um, Vern." Phil ogled the woman appreciatively. "Mila looks like that Spanish chick from the *Real World*. The one from Nic...Nico..."

"Nicaragua." They both watched Mila punch Vernon lightly. She had her hair up and was wearing a tight red dress. Erin could see the panty lines even from there. "Hit him harder, sweetheart. And lower."

"Hey, that's funny, Mrs. Night. You're being funny."

"Do you still want that light?" she asked, mercifully changing the subject. "I'll trade you fire for smoke." She grabbed a book of matches from the nearest table. "CN&W. A PERFECT 10" was written in silver leaf on its black cover.

How Phil hadn't seen them was indicative of his condition. He couldn't steady his hands to light the cigarette so she did it for him. Then she pulled it out of his mouth and took it for herself. "Ladies first," she said.

He didn't complain. As he got another cigarette, Phillip contemplated the still-attractive 41-year-old woman standing before him. He knew she was married to one of his bosses so he had to be cool. But he could also tell that she was wanting for something. Him maybe? Her eyes were these two drains just sucking in whatever material was around them. Two beautiful drains. "What's wrong, Mrs. Night? He asked. "You don't seem right."

"And you keep rhyming. I tell you what, I'll be Silent Bob and you play the rapper."

"You're funny pretty. I mean pretty funny."

"Call me Erin," she answered, unbothered by his drunken patter, remotely touched by his concern. "For one thing it's harder to rhyme than Mrs. Night. Not to mention less offensive."

Phil let her light his cigarette. "Okay, sure. Hi Erin."

"And you're Phil, right?"

"Phil Connors. At your service." He actually saluted. "You know you're awfully sexy when you smile."

"Well, I'll be damned!" exclaimed Erin. "I am smiling." She raised her champagne flute to his beer glass. "Here's to small pleasures and chance encounters. Wherever and whenever!"

Emboldened, Phil stepped in closer. "I like it when you're happy, Erin. I'd like to make you happier."

Amused to find herself being hit on by this drunken kid, in seconds Erin hatched a plan. "Would you like to make me really happy, Phillip? Insanely and voluptuously happy?"

"Oh, you know it. Of course I would."

"Splendid. Come over here. Closer. You see that man over there, in the suit I picked out for him, talking to the two girls from his harem?"

"You mean our President?"

"Hail to the chief!"

For some reason Phil whispered: "I see him but I don't think he sees us."

"No, he looks pretty busy. But listen, I want you to do something for me, Phillip. Something crazy funny. Okay?"

"Crazy funny. Or funny crazy? What do you have in mind?"

"I want you to push Vernon in the pool."

Phil assumed she was joking and laughed. He stood there smoking, waiting for her to change the subject. He polished off his rum punch.

"I'm serious." And she was. Seeing her husband drunkenly flail away in the pool suddenly seemed infinitely more satisfying than her sinking in some corner of it. Unlike suicide, it wouldn't ruin the party either.

"I don't think Vernon would like that, Erin." He laughed sheepishly. "I mean he'd get all wet."

Erin inched toward him. "Why don't we let me do all the thinking tonight, eh Phillip?" In a flirtatious gesture, she touched his nose. "Besides, I know he'll think it's funny. Voluptuously funny." Erin tilted, affording him a better view of her cleavage. "Trust me." She straightened his tie.

"But you're asking me to push my boss into a swimming pool. At a company party. His company party. That's crazy!"

She nodded gleefully. "Precisely. And that's what's so great about the idea. Everybody will get a kick out of it."

"Isn't that kind of harsh? I mean with clients here and everything."

"Nonsense. He'll look like a human being in front of the people. Not just a magazine cover, you know?"

"I don't know…"

But she had him. She just needed one more enticement, one more lie to close the deal. "We're guests at the hotel, Phil. He's got plenty of clothes he can change into." Purring now, "And I've got plenty of clothes I can change out of. Sound good?" She deposited a soft kiss on his lips.

Phil did not take long to make up his drunken, horny mind. He set down his stein, flicked his smoke into the shrubs, and purposefully began his march around the pool. When he reached his target, the entourage parted, surprised and irritated by the intrusion. Both men faced one another.

"I was talking here," said Vernon, annoyed.

"And now you're swimming." And with that Phil Connors pushed Vernon Night into the pool.

After the splash, there was a moment of total silence, not unlike before the woman screams in a horror movie. Everyone was stunned, especially Vernon.

He stood up best he could, considering he was in four feet of water. His mouth opened but nothing came out.

His $700 glasses finished breaking and fell from his face in two pieces. Vernon's PDA destructed immediately thereafter, emitting tiny but colorful explosions from inside of his now-ruined cashmere jacket. Possibly all the $100 bills he was going to pass out as anniversary gifts could be saved. But little else on him would make it.

With nearsighted eyes, Vernon located the perpetrator. Smiled weakly. Then spoke, words so obvious he almost need not have said them:

"Phil, you're fired."

ELEVEN

ALAN Robertson had a cluttered, messy office, filled with memorabilia and assorted souvenirs. A big man, with white hair and beard, Alan was not your typical Beverly Hills shrink. He was the spitting image of Santa Claus. Except this Santa wore a Notre Dame sweatshirt and khakis.

Vernon reclined on the patient's couch playing with a baseball. Alan repeated the question: "Let me get this straight. An employee pushed you in the pool simply because your wife asked him to?"

"Please, Alan, could you not repeat everything I say back to me as a question? You're like a voice-over that keeps harping on the price."

"Excuse me but this is an out-of-the-ordinary event," replied Robertson. He lit the cigar that he perpetually kept on his desk. Not only was Alan Robertson the only non-Jewish shrink in Beverly Hills, he was also the only smoker.

"I mean, you haven't requested an emergency session since your last affair went bust." Even though he knew Vernon didn't care, he clicked on his smoke-removing device. A force of habit, but in this town smoke was never taken in stride. Most of his patients abhorred it. As a matter of fact, one of them had given him the machine.

Vernon slid back in the chair, kneading the baseball pretty well. "So, I made a last-minute appointment. More money in your pocket."

"So, obviously, you're under duress," Dr. Robertson responded. His patient was going through a rough spot, this latest episode yet another downward turn in the spiral. About six months ago he'd begun noticing more swears in Vernon's speech, more vitriol. Barry wasn't just overrated anymore; now he was *clueless*. Erin had gone from being a pill to a bitch to a *goddamn cunt;* and now she was gone period. His increasingly venomous diatribes made him sound like Hitler in his bunker.

Whenever Alan had questioned him about it Vernon lashed out even more. "You're the fucking doctor," he'd say. "You tell me what the problem is."

At times, Alan even considered eliminating him as a client. In the end he couldn't. He still considered Vernon Night a salvageable prospect. "What happened after he pushed you in the water?" Alan asked, returning to the unfortunate incident.

"I got fucking wet," Vernon said.

"After that."

"I fired his sorry ass." Vernon said, smiling joylessly.

"How did that feel, firing him?"

"I don't know. It felt like it was supposed to feel."

The shrink remained quiet. He knew Vernon wasn't done answering the question. In Alan's view remaining silent during a session was the most important aspect of analysis. *Listening.* Nobody did it anymore. Or if they did they were only pretending. Alan Robertson got paid 275 dollars for 45 minutes to listen. And it was still tough. That's how hard listening was.

"I don't know. Maybe I deserved it…"

There we go.

"It's weird, Doc, but when I was under water – for that split second – that's what I was thinking. That I deserved being pushed." Vernon grimaced. He stared at all the miscellaneous crap that was collecting on his shrink's desk: The miniature Statue of Liberty. The Altoids tin. The same dead cactus. "The wheels are coming off, aren't they?"

"Maybe. Maybe not." But Robertson sensed an opportunity. "Vernon, if I ask you a question will you promise to give me a thoughtful answer?"

"No."

Recognizing his client's humor, or lack thereof, Alan proceeded: "Where is the hatred coming from?"

Vernon grabbed the Statue of Liberty and checked its base. "Made in Cambodia." He dropped it on the floor.

"Anger. Even now I can feel it."

"What? That piece of crap. Who cares? I'll buy you another one." Vernon crossed his arms and legs. Stared nowhere.

Alan got out of his chair and picked up the statue. He placed the trinket back on his desk. A patient who'd come to America against her will had given it to him. Lots of patients gave him things. His desktop was an altar. While he was moving he kept his eyes on his client. Everything transpiring right now was part of therapy.

Vernon felt cornered, like being under water. "I don't know why I threw your statue on the floor." Vernon said, turning away. "Something just comes over me. I get mad. I don't know. Whatever."

Their time was nearly up but they were making headway. If only he didn't have Mrs. Crowe right behind him. Alan knew she was out there, already waiting. "I'm sorry Vernon but I don't allow 'whatever' in here. That's a kid's expression."

"Look Doc, I'm sorry I sound like a kid to you but I'm forty fucking years old and I'm angry. I feel like punching somebody. I don't know why." He rubbed his temple. "You know, I make a lot of money and I've achieved a lot of things. I make more money than the President of the United States. I make more money than you." He paused. "Sorry."

Alan looked him in the eye, the unlit cigar still in his mouth. "You wouldn't believe how many of my patients say the very same thing. As if having lots of money means you won't have any problems."

"What can I tell you? If I didn't have any money I couldn't afford you. Then what's left? Church. Prayers. Whatever. Unfortunately I don't believe in God. Jesse Ventura was right. Organized religion is for the simple minded."

"I believe Karl Marx said it first."

Vernon checked his watch. "Time's up, right?"

Alan sighed. "Both inside and outside forces can cause a person to be angry. Your wife had some drunk push you in a pool, an angry gesture too, and naturally it pissed you off. But while that may have been a catalyst for your anger I think you've been experiencing varying degrees of rage for quite some time. You're unusually hostile. To your colleagues, to your partner, to me...and now, of all things, to *God*."

"And let me guess, it's stemming from something inside me. Some inner demon or what-." He stopped himself from saying "whatever."

"Look, Vernon, I know it sounds painfully obvious. You've achieved much but something is missing. This makes you angry. Now we have something to work on!" He stood up indicating their session was over. "I'll see you at our regular hour."

"Meantime," Vernon added, "I'll need a refill on my Xanax."

MRS. CROWE BEAMED at Vernon when he passed her in the waiting room. "Hello Vernon, how are you?"

"Going downhill fast. How about you?" he replied sarcastically. He hated that she insisted on greeting him, knew his name. But then he hated that he *hated*. What was his problem? He considered offering the old woman an apology but opted to just keep walking.

Few old office buildings like this one stood in L.A. The lone elevator took forever arriving. And nothing was more annoying than waiting for an elevator. Vernon stared at his reflection in the grimy doors pondering his newly diagnosed rage.

Alan had him though. It wasn't Erin, Barry, or somebody else's fault. Something inside was causing him to foment. Earlier he'd said he felt like a volcano ready to blow. But standing there, in the forlorn, musty hallway, he thought of a more appropriate analogy: It was like he had this sewer inside and it was chronically backing up. Bile could be defined as an ill-humored state or a bitter greenish fluid secreted from within. What bile was inside of him creating all this vitriol?

What he could discern of his reflection looked like Hell. Vernon sighed. He took pride in his physical appearance, the haircut and the clothes, the whole package. Could a polluted mind corrupt the body? He thought about the saved porn sites on his computer and how he wallowed in them. The prostitutes. The drinking. His divorce. Clearly, bitter fluid was seeping onto the surface.

The lift rattled along, an apt metaphor for Vernon's state of mind. Since the pool party incident he no longer resided at home. He'd gotten a great weekly rate on a suite at, of all places, the Four Seasons! If nothing else, there were people from the biz there, including now a potential client.

Vernon hadn't pestered Barry yet about how things were going on Happy Soul. Not that it would do much good. Creatives like Barry were sensitive. God forbid you trampled on their newly forming concepts. They never had anything to show until the last minute anyway, a constant source of frustration for him and all the other account guys. The bickering between creative and suit was endemic to the business, so inevitable it had become a cliché.

THINGS WERE AT a standstill on the freeway. In a black mood, no way Vernon was enduring traffic. He grabbed a partially dressed blow-up doll from the back seat, depositing her next to him. With his fake companion, Vernon veered into the carpool lane.

He put in the CD of *Rubber Soul*, his favorite Beatles album. Paul McCartney began singing about places he remembered. Vernon wondered if he even had a soul? Lewdly, the doll fell into Vernon's lap. It would be nice, he thought, pushing her back, if the Happy Soul

Industry were for real. Going one step further, what if creating ads on behalf of goodness created goodness in general? Could one repair a fetid sewer by whitewashing the sink? He doubted it. The inflatable woman found his lap again. Despite winning awards, their PSAs for the local 'Y' hadn't pulled in many donations. Happy Soul Industry had its work cut out, as would the agency should it become a client. Still, if a creative solution existed Barry would find it. Engaging his Bluetooth, he got his partner on the line. "Did we crack the code on Happy Soul?"

"We? It's been one day, Vern."

"That long?" At this point, he and the love doll were having a relationship, albeit a challenging one.

"I'm checking in on Irma right now." Irma was a Senior Art Director. Vernon heard Barry walking as he talked.

"You put Irma on it? I'd like to put Irma on *it*."

Barry sighed. "I've got Human Resources on speakerphone."

Vernon sang: "She's a very funky girl…"

"Where are you?"

"Coming back from the shrink."

"You coming in?"

"Not sure," Vernon said. "I need to stop at Walgreens. You got something to show me?"

"Irma said she's got something."

Vernon laughed. "I bet."

"Say, Vern, while you're at the drug store get yourself some salt-peter."

"And discourage my libido?" He pinched the plastic woman's boob. "Never!"

"I've got ads to make," Barry said, hanging up.

Vernon exited the freeway. The opening strings to *Norwegian Wood* began filling the vehicle. "I once had a girl…" He sang along to the girl sitting next to him. The gravity of his earlier encounter with Alan had vanished. The truly Big Questions would have to wait. Now he was singing to a sex toy.

TWELVE

BARRY worked the art directors like a rooster in a hen house, marching from office to office, delivering criticism and providing inspiration. Although staff would probably never admit it, they vied for his attention like a jealous harem.

But Barry felt less than cocky. He hadn't created the Big Idea. So now he had to find it. On the surface the Happy Soul Industry was a dream client: A seemingly great business run by a seemingly great guy. Word had gotten out and everyone in the agency wanted in on the pitch. But it was to Irma's office he headed.

While African Americans held numerous positions at Chloe Night, some in high places, the creative department remained a bastion of young, white males. Irma was the lone exception. Barry had been delighted to find her, both to satisfy California's ever-stricter hiring laws and, more importantly, because it was *right*. Diversity was correct, beyond just politically.

As evidence of the status quo's shortcomings mounted, so did the number of dissatisfied clients and consumers. It became increasingly important finding staff from previously untapped resources.

More than one client questioned why the agency hadn't opened an "urban affiliate." Spike Lee had his Joint at DDB. The Leo Burnett Company formed an outpost called Vigilante. Yet he and Vernon had declined. Vernon because he was Vernon: "I'm not giving a black person a job because it's trendy!"

And Barry because Vernon, behind the bluster, had a point: Creating an African American agency was a heartfelt yet brain-dead idea. Hiring blacks specifically to speak to blacks only separated them further from the rest of society, the results often worse than the racism that spawned it. So no urban Joint for Chloe Night. They would continue to hire only the most capable people, regardless of gender or creed.

Barry admired Irma's office. Unlike his own chaotic workspace, the Senior Art Director kept her room immaculate, from the shiny white Mac to her artfully arranged photographs of famous black artists and writers.

At 30 years old, Irma was poised for her age. Graceful, her hair in a stylish roll, she wore a Donna Karan suit, the faint aroma of Chanel No. 5 reinforcing her understated classicism. Barry thought she art-directed herself as well as she art-directed ads. They'd made a good choice hiring Irma.

With Irma lost in thought, Barry had to cough to get her attention.

"Any luck?"

"Have a look."

Instead of turning to greet her boss, she swiveled the monitor for him to see. On screen was a template of a typical bus shelter, her work representing the ad found within it. In an elegant typeface she'd written the client's name, lower case: **happy soul industry**. Above it resided the headline, a simple question: **How are you?**

"How...Are...You?" Barry read the question twice.

"Simple question, right?" Irma continued: "We all ask it. Every-day. Dozens of times."

Indeed, it was perhaps the most common question in the world, so mundane it had essentially lost all meaning. Yet, presented in the context of a bus stop ad, something marvelous and unexpected happened: The once rhetorical question became an emotional clarion.

Barry rubbed his whiskers, brightened. "Everyone says 'How are you?' but what if we really meant it?"

"Exactly!" Irma beamed. "If we all really cared about one another, then Happy Soul Industry would be getting somewhere. We all would!"

Barry got it. Wanted to love it. Needed more proof. "Did you try playing with your idea, beyond just the theme?"

"Way ahead of you," she said, clicking her mouse, revealing another execution.

It had the same simple look, new headline: **These days, every-body's skipping prayer. So, how's everybody doing?** "We run messages like these on train platforms, bus stops; you know, places where people are stressed out, waiting to go to work."

Barry nodded quietly, the best sign if you knew him. He was not a talkative creative director but that didn't mean he wasn't captivated. "Make the worker bees stop and think," mused Barry. "I like it."

Excited, Irma continued her presentation. "And look how it works in the daily paper. This is the business section, next to the stock reports." She showed him a mock-up of a newspaper ad. The message: **Remember, you can't take it with you.**

Barry laughed. "That would be cool next to the obits as well."

He sparked to the theme, relishing the idea of imbuing shopworn phrases with new and powerful meanings, which, by the way, was the definition of copywriting.

"Have you thought about how the idea works in television?" His wheels were definitely turning. He'd seen a glimpse and now he wanted more. Could the idea work across media?

"Maybe we don't do television, Barry," Irma answered, bravely.

She knew television was the king of all media. Suggesting they needn't use it would raise eyebrows internally, considering the open budget.

But what made Irma's notion truly provocative was the fact that a reel put writers and art directors on the creative map. If you had a few great spots in your portfolio you could double your salary. Print, no matter how beautifully crafted, could not catapult a career like TV.

However, Irma wasn't being selfish. She had her concept in mind. "These words lose their meaning when spoken. For some reason it feels more personal in writing."

Barry hated walking away from television (the agency got better pub from TV as well as more operating profit) but he found Irma's argument compelling. Speak to the people not with a voice but in words. More often than not TV spoke at people, not to them. In this respect commercials were like proverbial thieves in the night, prying into your home, trying to take your money, and then slipping into the void.

Print was a written contract with the consumer. Literally. If done well print gave the advertiser a kind of integrity its showboat brother seldom possessed. One of CN&W's writers had an anecdote from his days at Leo Burnett: On every piece of office stationery was written "Do not give or receive oral instruction." Although the saying was eventually scrapped (probably for its inadvertent sexual connotation), Irma loved it. Television was *oral instruction* and therefore more prone to be false, a better liar. For Happy Soul, TV felt inappropriate.

"Well, let's not rule anything out just yet," Barry said, getting back to the business at hand, sounding like a good manager. "But I like where this is going, I really do. Did you try working with any colors?"

Irma had no intention of refuting her boss repeatedly, but: "Given we're basically advertising Heaven, I kind of liked the idea of only using white space."

"So you think Heaven is all white?"

"Watch it, Bar. You're beginning to sound like your partner!"

But she wasn't offended. She knew Barry was joking. Plus he had a point. Heaven was, indeed, usually portrayed as white on white. They shared a laugh, giddy over the idea in the room. "Say Bar, did the client give us any identity work? A logo? I mean, what color scheme are they using now?"

"I don't know." Barry paused, surprised by his answer. "Come to think of it, they didn't give us anything."

Most clients came to them with numerous equities as well as baggage: a failed ad campaign, a clumsy tag line, at least some business cards! But not the Happy Soul Industry.

"I think they wanted to see what we're made of." Barry said.

Irma shrugged. "I think they want to see what all of us are made of."

THIRTEEN

FRUSTRATED by traffic on the Santa Monica Freeway, Vernon elected to exit early and take surface streets. Ostensibly, he was looking for a Walgreens closer to the hotel. But should he exit La Brea or La Cienega? Like everyone else in L.A., Vernon wasn't a native and often its streets confused him, remaining as foreign as the language they were named in. At 70 miles per hour, his befuddlement was only compounded. He chose La Brea.

He chose wrong. Bisecting Hollywood and Beverly Hills, this far south La Brea had little in common with either. Hardly a ghetto, but Vernon wasn't seeing many stars either. This was commercial L.A. Dingy and dirty. He noticed wrecked buildings, devastated by the earthquake and riots from over a decade earlier. Years had gone by and yet no one had repaired them.

Realizing he had passed the drugstore, Vernon pulled over to the curb in preparation for a U-turn. He rolled down his window to spit his chewing gum. Bad move. For at that moment a revolver entered the vehicle. It was attached to an impatient young man.

"Okay, Mister, it's like this," the assailant said. "I'm getting in the car and you're going to start driving." He did not wait for a reply. This was not a conversation. "Unlock the fucking doors!"

Astonished this was happening in broad daylight, on a busy street, yet not at all surprised it was happening to him, Vernon released the door latches.

The phrase "par for the course" came to mind. If anything, being accosted by a gun-toting thug was exactly how the script should go, the latest wicked turn in the downward spiral of Vernon Night.

The young man kept his gun pointed at Vernon as he moved to the passenger side and got in the car, shoving up against the inflatable doll. "Go!" he said. "Make a U when you can."

"Um, about the girl, she's for the carpool lane." Vernon had to comment. God forbid his assailant think he's a weirdo.

"Just drive, asshole!" The thief threw the plastic woman in the back seat.

Vernon did as he was told, evoking a slew of honks entering traffic.

Didn't they notice he'd just been carjacked? Vernon suspected actors late for a casting call. Everyone in L.A was so fucking self-absorbed.

The duo headed up La Brea toward the mostly smog-covered hills. Vernon could barely discern the first part of Hollywood's most famous sign. It read HOLL but it looked like HELL. He wondered why his assailant didn't just take the vehicle. Vernon made the U-turn. Of course there were no police to catch him doing that. "Where to?" he asked.

"Freeway."

"East or West?" Vernon asked, making an effort to be civil. Again he got no immediate answer from the gunman. Vernon cleared his throat. They were approaching the on-ramps. He tried a variation. "Right or left?"

The gunman said nothing. "I'm not sure."

"Well, where is it you want to go?"

More silence, then: "Disneyland."

"Excuse me?"

For the first time, Vernon looked at the man sitting beside him and noticed that he was hardly a man at all. He looked all of seventeen. The Dodgers cap he wore made him appear even younger, partially concealing his brown, almond-shaped eyes. He had dark skin and black hair. A year or two ago and Vernon's probably taking him home to his mommy. The gun belied the young man's age. Guns had that kind of power. They made men juvenile and juveniles men.

"I said Disneyland. Now start driving, Holmes, or you're going straight to Hell!"

Vernon made the appropriate turn, east. Obviously he was in danger, but Disneyland? From what Vernon could tell his assailant wasn't on drugs. He couldn't see any gang tattoos crawling up his slim arms either. *Just the gun, just the gun.*

"Actually, I'm not sure where Disneyland is," Vernon lied, conjuring strategy. If he didn't know where to go then chances are they might stop. Stopping could provide an opportunity for escape or help of some kind. If he asked about a cell phone, it was still at the bottom of the Four Seasons pool.

"Come on, Holmes, everybody knows where Disneyland is."

"You didn't," Vernon said, sheepishly. He managed a tiny smile. "You wouldn't shoot a man for being stupid?"

The kid seethed. "Pull into that drive-through." He pointed to a Taco-Laco restaurant coming up on the right.

"You're hungry... *Now?*" Oh, the irony, Vernon thought as he pulled into the driveway of his biggest client. He'd had to go there against his will before but never at gunpoint.

"Get directions. Nothing funny, right Holmes?"

"Welcome to Taco-Laco. Would you like to try a Bandito Burrito?" It was a simple request, ludicrous coming out of a huge, plastic chihuahua. It crackled again for their order. Barry was right. The talking dog was getting old.

The carjacker hollered: "Two of them. And two chimis with extra sauce!"

So he was hungry? Like any kid, Vernon figured he'd eaten here way too many times. The talking dog asked if they wanted beans. "No fork food," the car thief answered. "I'm holding a gun."

"Speak up, please!" the dog demanded.

Vernon completed the order, also requesting directions to the famous theme park. He had his doubts but the dog knew! He barked them out along with the total: "Four-fifty. Pull up for your items."

Service issues aside, Vernon had to hand it to his client. They were cheap. No wonder it was so popular. A family of eight could get out of there for less than ten bucks. And there were a lot of families of eight in Southern California.

Back on the freeway, both men ate their burritos quietly, one also holding a gun, the other the wheel. Vernon broke the silence, introducing himself: "My name is Vernon. What's yours?"

"I can't tell you."

"Make one up then. I've got to call you something."

The young man considered the request. "Luis. My name is Luis."

"You know, Luis," continued Vernon. "I make all the TV commercials for Taco-Laco."

"The talking dog? For real?"

"That's right, Luis," bragged Vernon. "I thought of him myself."

"You're lucky I don't shoot you right now." Luis imitated the dog's whiny TV voice: "Mira! Mira! Mira! You know how offensive that is?"

"Hey, that's not fair!" Vernon shouted. "We got two Silver Slippers for that campaign."

"I don't give a shit what you got. No excuse for putting down my race. We don't go around yipping and yapping like clowns."

"What?" Vernon feigned ignorance. *But he knew*. A columnist from *The New York Times* had recently called the Taco-Laco dog the most racially offensive advertising critter since the Frito Bandito.

Vernon regarded the slim teenager with the big silver gun. He was actually a very handsome young man and, despite the crime he was committing, seemingly an intelligent one. "I'm sorry," Vernon said. What else could he say?

The teen nodded. "It's all right, man." He sighed. "Besides, my sister loves that dog. But then she also loves that puta, Ricky Martin." He scratched his cheek with the revolver. Then grimaced. "Mira! Mira! Mira! What were you thinking?"

"It means look," Vernon said, embarrassed.

"Hey Holmes, I know what the word means." Luis shook his head. "And why don't you look where you're going?" He waved the gun again, lest Vernon forget who was calling the shots. "How about a little less conversation and more transportation?"

The line came from a popular action picture. Not long ago Vernon actually used it on his wife. If he recalled correctly, she'd told him to go fuck himself.

"Why are we going to Disneyland, Luis?"

Luis stopped eating. "We was supposed to go," he said, growing somber. "My brother and me. We'd won the tickets from my church. But then my brother got himself shot in a drive-by. Game over."

"Jesus. Is he all right?"

"Yeah, he's okay. But now he's in jail. Four years."

"Sorry to hear that, Luis. I really am."

"Ain't nothing, Holmes. Ain't nothing."

Both men ate in quiet.

FOURTEEN

WHEN David opened his eyes the first thing he noticed was Evelyn's side of the bed, empty and cool. "How could she have gotten by me?" He wondered aloud. "I'm supernatural. I don't even sleep!" He rolled over to find the clock. Nearly nine. *Had he really been sleeping that long? Had he really been sleeping?* Too many questions. But here was a woman whose life he'd nearly ended, then saved, and now slept with. More could not have happened between two people in a lifetime, let alone 24 hours.

And now she was gone.

David mulled over current events: The bar, the Ivy and the drive into the hills. It had all gone so well, better than any date he could remember having had in his life. And what about the events *after the date*, here in this room, in this very bed? David could smell her on the pillow. He sighed. They'd made love three times, each time being better than before. He'd never known physical pleasure like that, or even if it existed. David was certain Evelyn had felt the same way. Certain.

But now she was gone.

Evelyn's absence had to be logical. Maybe she had an early business meeting. Or perhaps she was swimming. David sprung from the bed, somersaulting once before his feet touched the carpet. He stretched, as a live man would, felt his muscles pull and bones crack. As a live man would, he also felt vulnerable. Naked.

Summoning his robe, he wrapped himself in it. David believed his wife had done him a favor marrying him. He never discussed these insecurities with anyone (including her), but they'd plagued him for the duration of his marriage. Upon arrival into Heaven, he'd checked these sorts of wraps at the door. No doubts, fears, or feelings of inadequacy need haunt him ever again. So why were they now?

Suddenly the anxiety manifested itself as a feral creature! The animal raced around the room, ripping and tearing at the furniture, raising hell.

David jumped out of its path and onto the bed. The mongoose – if that's what it was – hissed at him, its red eyes glaring. The small beast dug his long claws into the carpet, easily shredding it.

David had been warned about such manifestations. God said they happened to angels when they rejoined the living, during times of panic or stress. One wasn't to engage the beasts. Rather treat them for what they were originally, she'd instructed. Do as you would if you were mortal and in mental pain. Start exercising or have a martini. Prayer helped, obviously.

Easy for God to say!

The creature snarled as it approached.

In life, David had been prone to panic attacks. He knew what to do. He closed his eyes, took deep breaths, and, out loud, counted to ten with each exhale. A simple procedure but it worked.

Right away the animal responded. In circles it ran, chasing its tail. Faster and faster the little beast wheeled until almost a blur. Halfway through David's count, the manifestation shot under the bed.

But was it gone or merely hiding?

"Damnation," David said, uttering his first cuss word in ages, albeit an archaic one.

He slid off the bed slowly, one leg at a time.

As an angel, he'd forgotten how awful mental anguish could be. Supernatural manifestations aside, David struggled comprehending how he, or the current population, had managed with psychosis at all.

Yet, if he remembered correctly, periods of mental illness were common. David imagined new medicines existed to counteract these rogue feelings, but he was skeptical of their value, just as he had been a century ago, when a physician had, in fact, prescribed him various opiates for his occasional "spells."

Thinking about it now, he regretted not seeing an alienist back then. But psychiatry was seldom practiced. The circus fortuneteller had more credibility.

David composed himself, checking under the bed once more to be sure.

The vermin had thankfully disappeared but, ode to joy, not so his lover's underthings! David picked up the black panties, bringing them to his face. He sniffed. Like a bloodhound the memory of her overtook him completely. David's legs grew wobbly. He could not suppress a moan. Overwhelmed by emotions, he rose carefully, attempting to steady himself by leaning on the bed.

The Chloe Night presentation wasn't until 3 p.m., which meant that he had nearly six hours to kill. He would have loved spending every second with Evelyn but obviously that wasn't going to happen.

David let the panties fall to the floor. Then his robe. He stepped away from the garments, moving toward the room's center.

Unlike yesterday, David didn't feel like taking an earthly shower. He would cleanse the heavenly way. A bristling halo of kinetic energy appeared over his head before descending around David, and scrubbed him clean. He held his arms aloft, allowing his body to be ministered to; much as a shark does with the tiny sea wrasse.

Clean now, David put on his robe, then floated toward the sliding glass doors, which opened for him, taking him onto the balcony. He hovered within its modest perimeter. He didn't require oxygen to live but he hoped the fresh air would at least clear his head.

Gazing upon West Hollywood, he watched the morning haze collect in some areas while burning off in others. The aroma of coffee from the outdoor restaurant mingled with other breakfast smells. He detected bougainvillea as well. David fixated on a woman walking her dog on the street below. She had long brown hair and, even from the terrace he could tell, a fine figure. He missed Evelyn.

Restless, he went back into the room. David did what most of the population did when it was anxious, bored or restless: He turned on the television.

A lady reporter was describing a calamity, fire and smoke erupting behind her. Precariously, she stood on the rickety steps of an ancient, and now heavily damaged monastery. Thick black smoke billowed from its windows. The reporter constantly held an arm up, deflecting burning ash or worse.

David appreciated the gothic lines of the structure. But it was obvious much of the detail was gone, having been obliterated. He played with the remote, discovering the volume control. She spoke:

"More bombs fell this morning, this time wrecking the Church of Naviticus, a significant building dating from the seventeenth century." The reporter said all this while walking up the few remaining, crumbling stairs. She then thought better of it and returned to its base.

"This was a primary place of worship in the community," she reported. After a dramatic pause: "How long will these beleaguered people continue to have their faith tested?"

Shocked and transfixed by what he was seeing, David fell to his knees in front of the television. How could a place of worship have been so desecrated? Did not the warring tribes respect one another's temples?

As if answering his questions the reporter continued: "In a statement released earlier today, General Jolosovic claimed the bombing was an accident of war. As you might imagine, his detractors were furious, asserting that the dictator had purposefully destroyed their church."

Hardly naïve, David was all too familiar with the horrors of war. In his time, right and wrong were black and white. One obeyed God's rules or broke them, the latter easily leading to violence. Intolerance and unjust prosecution in the name of God had become common-place. Sadly, organized religion was less about peace than a touch-stone for conflict.

And so here it was again. He listened to the newswoman sum up the bleak events. Stunningly, a segment followed describing the vari-ous missiles used in the conflict, including the one believed to have taken out the church in the story.

David easily remembered his generation's epic conflict. World War I had been the first conflagration that featured machines. He recalled watching a train roll by, its cargo of silver cannon shells relentlessly moving east toward the harbors of New York. Pictures of bombed churches had been in the papers then as well. That war would eventu-ally obliterate the last vestiges of Victoriana just as sure as the rocket on TV had blown up that church. Which was worse: watching it now or the fact that he'd seen it all before?

Another newsman began discussing body counts, the ratios between women and men, even children. The reporter seemed unmoved by the content of his message. It's not that David expected him to weep, but he didn't even blink.

When David had processed insurance claims, his heart broke eas-ily for those clients and their hardships. How were these TV people remaining so cool? David wondered if hearts became chilled by a daily parade of sorrow. He prayed not. Finally, and mercifully, the piece ended.

But then came the commercials.

And in their own way David found them more obscene. Not because of what they were about – banks and cars and video games – but because of how blindly they went about their business.

Like the reporters, the spots traipsed across the screen utterly unaware of their context. He likened the gaudy assemblage to jugglers and minstrels providing the Devil distraction.

Death and Pain will be right back...but first a word from our sponsor!

An advertisement for a video game called *Doom Slayer* felt particularly inappropriate. The object of the game was avoiding annihilation by Satan's minions. Relentless zombie-like creatures grabbed for your flesh, devouring it. To survive, one had to pump lead into their fevered brains. Each kill entitled you to more ammunition. Yet, there were always more creatures. The tag line for *Doom Slayer*: "War is Hell. Have a Nice Day!"

David had enough. God hadn't prepared him for carnage as gamesmanship!

He thrust his fist into the television's glass face, pulling out its fizzling, exploding guts. He held the television's vital organs with both hands and actually felt them die.

A wisp of blue smoke arose from the mechanical debris, not unlike the way a person's soul departed from the body.

Observing the acrid plume, he became even more distressed, and threw the handful of debris into a corner, ruining carpet and walls.

David sat down on the edge of his bed and cried. He recited the Lord's Prayer, followed by the Serenity Prayer.

Yesterday he danced on water. Last night he made love to a gorgeous woman. Now he was having a breakdown. In the background, the disemboweled television sputtered.

What was going on?

The angel pined for Heaven's tranquility as he had just pined for Evelyn.

"I know TV lacks quality but show some restraint!" Evelyn strolled in like she'd been gone ten minutes. She set down a bag of groceries and surveyed the room. "So lover, what's going on here?'

Startled to see her, but weary, David shook his head. "Bad morning," he said. "What can I say?"

"Let me guess. You were upset I was gone." She smiled, impetuously. "Am I right?"

"Yes," David answered. "I was very upset. I thought maybe I had disappointed you in some way." He blushed, doubtful that his explanation accounted for the hotel room's condition. "I guess I got carried away."

"I like a man with passion." Evelyn replied.

She began removing items from the bag. "I got us some goodies. You haven't had deli until you've had *Nate & Al.*" She put out an assortment of bagels, smoked fish, and assorted other foodstuffs onto the small table next to his bed. "Hmmm, hmmm," Evelyn sang, happy as a jaybird.

Surprised that Evelyn had brushed off the devastation, he was also quite embarrassed so he let the matter go.

"The only thing missing are the scrambled eggs and onions," Evelyn chortled. "We could order some from room service. Would you like that?"

"It's not necessary," said David, speaking softly.

He stared at Evelyn's hands as she set up their breakfast, marveling at her appetites, her indifference to the chaos. She seemed business as usual, beautiful as ever. Had he imagined the mongoose, the ruined church, his rage?

"I know you're seeing that other agency this afternoon," she said, "but I was hoping we could spend the day together. Or at least the morning."

She gazed at him intensely, pursing her lips, blowing him a kiss. Evelyn placed a few strips of the finely cut salmon into her mouth, rolling the pink fish on her tongue.

"But first I say we eat and then do it like bunnies!"

"What are your plans today?" asked David, coveting her once again.

"After you...focus groups." Evelyn laughed. "I made the arrangements this morning."

Wiping away the last vestige of his tears, he put his arms around her waist. He had no idea what focus groups were but if Evelyn was going he wanted to as well.

"First things first," he replied, giving her a kiss.

FIFTEEN

"THE human mind is our number one enemy," the Humanologist said, trying to attach the e-meter to Mila's head. One of the clips wasn't holding and both student and teacher were getting frustrated.

"Call me crazy," Mila said, "but how is using your head a bad thing, I mean without this thing stuck to it?"

A pivotal auditing session for Mila, her advancement to the next level depended on it. Yet her interviewer, Jane, was grating on her nerves. Jane was one of those people who peppered her speech with sound bites and catch phrases, especially those from the Church of Humanology. "We've been through this before. Rationalization is a crime against progress. *Your progress.*"

Mila knew the drill: Follow the rules and everything would be fine. But now she was struggling with the dogma, not to mention the chinstraps. "Ouch!" she barked.

"Look, it's natural for you to fight the process. The rational mind does not want you to reach a higher plane."

"I suppose but..." Mila had spent all this time (and money) trying to better herself and now the Church was asking her stop *thinking* about it. She wanted so much to achieve clarity. But she had her doubts about the auditing process, about turning it all over.

Jane was relentless: "It's natural for you to fight the process. Smart children rebel against their parents." She'd witnessed defensiveness like Mila's in countless others, especially at this stage of development, where a student either advanced to practitioner or bailed out. Up to a third of the initiates opted for the latter but Jane counted on this one to make it. Mila had done well in previous sessions. It would be a shame to lose her now.

Jane managed to get one of the straps to hold. "Remember, Mila, the reactive mind is the enemy of Humanology."

"Humanology has a lot of enemies, doesn't it?" She'd come this far. How many levels now – three, four? And how many dollars had she spent? This interview alone had cost her 350. The Church might be saving her from failure and compromise but it wasn't doing anything good for her bank account. Yet, Jane wasn't a monster, an enemy. She genuinely wanted Mila to achieve her goals, and clarity.

The second strap broke in her hands.

"I'll tell you what, Mila," Jane said, putting the ungainly contraption under the table. "Let's not use the meter. I think you're ready for some eye work."

"Eye work?"

Her eyes were fine. Mila rightly assumed that "eye work" was yet another coded expression. The Church always held back information or parceled it out in tiny, coded phrases. Everything was bestowed on a need-to-know basis.

And Mila's treatment was no exception. Every time she'd been led to a new facility it was always dark when they got there. And there was always a new facility. When she asked about Humanology's covert practices she got more of the same in response, another evasive answer, a slogan.

Humanology sold information and there was no way it was going to be dispensed via buffet. Limited data output, coupled with a high degree of confidentiality, ensured that the outside world stayed outside. Humanology was impossibly tight-lipped about its doctrine as well as with the goings-on behind closed doors. The fact that Mila had no idea what "eye work" meant was a perfect example.

Jane opened up. "It's an advanced procedure. Only Level 5 and above. But I think you're ready. Do you feel ready to emerge from your pupa, Mila Rodriguez?"

Without waiting for an answer, Jane gave Mila a hot towel, a solution-filled dropper, and a small blue pill. "Take the pill. Wash your face. Put two drops in each eye." These weren't questions.

Mila eyed the pill suspiciously. "I thought we were forbidden to use drugs?"

"It's medicine, Mila. A common relaxant. Let's proceed."

Mila trusted her. She took the pill.

"Good girl!" When Mila completed her instructions, Jane removed the towel along with Mila's purse and other incidentals. She wanted a clean, distraction-free environment. "Okay, Mila, I need to ask you an important question."

Mila nodded, tentatively. She felt woozy. Could the pill already be taking effect? Impossible. Maybe it was nerves.

Jane kept talking. "Are you ready to let go of the reactive mind that keeps you blind? Would you like some clarity in your life? Would you like to be able to see what others cannot?"

"That's a lot of questions."

"But you need only give one answer: Yes!"

"Yes."

"These are for you, Mila." Jane handed her a small black, velvet covered box. The Humanology insignia was emblazoned on its top. "They are extremely delicate so handle them carefully."

Slowly, Mila opened the fancy container. She reached in and pulled out what looked like a pair of... "Toothpicks?"

"Hardly," Jane scoffed. "These tools were designed specifically for this drill by the Creator himself!"

The Creator was a commercial illustrator and painter from the 1950s. He'd drawn lurid covers for science-fiction books and comics. How he'd created Humanology (let alone its "tools") was as incredible a story as anything found in a comic book. Just as amazing was how many people bought into it.

Mila contemplated the small sticks. "Drill?" she asked. "I thought we were only *looking*." Shuddering, Mila grew lightheaded.

"We are going to put one in each eye, just under your top and bottom lid," prompted Jane.

"It will prevent you from blinking which prevents us from thinking. The reactive mind fades, as your eyes remain open. You will glimpse the truth. You will see the truth, Mila!"

"Wha?" Mila fidgeted. Jane was speaking in tongues.

"Oh Mila! This is your chance to reach Level 5! I know you can do it. Jack Lord knows you can do it. You know you can do it…"

"Jack Lord?" Mila was woozy. "I didn't know he was a Humanologist. Why did you say Jack Lord?"

"Put them in your eyes, Mila. Do it. Do it now!"

Mila picked up the little silver sticks. Each had rounded ends, presumably to keep one's eyelid from puncturing. Under the influence of drugs, Jane, and the Church, Mila placed the smooth end of each stick under her eyelids, over her eyes.

"It hurts."

"I know it does, Mila. Now listen to me. I want you to look at me and listen. Listen to me and look. Look at me and listen. Listen to me and look." Jane repeated the phrases over and over.

She held Mila's chin between her fingers. Their eyes were inches apart.

"I'm looking. I'm listening."

"Try harder! Yes, that's it. As you see me you must learn to look at others. Do not hide from them. Then you will see yourself. It's the only way."

Of all things, Mila suddenly thought of Vernon. He had everything. He'd even had her. Yet he was so unhappy. Humanology offered solutions that prestige and power could not. Proven solutions. It had to work.

"It's all getting so bright."

Mila's eyes hurt in ways she'd never experienced before. Once, she'd had a bad reaction to chlorine. And then hot wax splattered from a candle, landing in her eye. Those experiences were painful but familiar, part of the real world, an accident.

This was different. Her eyes dried. It was as if they were two pebbles lying in the desert. Mila moaned.

"Look at me and listen. Listen to me and look." Jane was in her face. "Look at me and listen. Listen to me and look." She kept repeating the words.

"Goddamn, Goddamn, Goddamn..." Mila blubbered but she couldn't stop looking into the other woman's eyes. "So bright. My eyes are burning!"

"That's it, Mila! It's called the new light. Look at me in the new light! You're getting it, Mila! Oh yes, you're receiving now. Take advantage. Look at me. See clearly. See me. See yourself. SEE!"

And so Mila saw. She saw another human being in a way she'd never seen one before.

According to Humanology, visceral eye contact broke down the barriers of personal space. Insecurities and anxieties broke down along with it. If you connected with another human in this way then you could be rid of your fears forever. The "Eye Job" made it impossible to see the same way again.

And so Mila saw. "I can see! I can see!" Mila sobbed.

Jane spoke: "You may remove the silver from your eyes."

Mila removed the objects, unaware of the bleeding. She was elated. She was high. She hugged Jane effusively.

"Congratulations, Mila. At Level 5, you can truly see people now. And they can see you. The *better* you."

Mila gasped. "I'm so happy I could cry..." But, in fact, she could not as her eyes were too dry to manufacture the tears.

SIXTEEN

SAMMY jumped on Barry's desk as he heated the bowl, splattering his dose, half cooked, all over the tabletop.

Shocked, Barry could only stare at the unusable globules of heroin while they seeped into his papers. He swiped the miniscule puddles, licking his shaking fingers. A futile gesture, Barry knew his habit required more than a drop on the tongue.

Pushing his cat away, Barry couldn't yell at the animal. Waking his family would only make matters worse.

Panicking, he rifled through his junk drawer searching for junk. He found just enough for another fix.

Bemused, the cat watched its owner cook a second bowl and tie off again.

Barry removed the small needle from its hermetically sealed envelope, filling it with drugs. His arm was beginning to show tracks since he'd graduated from snorting, something he swore he'd never do.

Fixed, Barry settled into his couch, pulling the quilt his mother gave him up to his chin. Eyes fluttering, body warmed by the hug of heroin, he drifted back to the office Christmas party three years ago...

It had been a banner year, capped off by winning the Path Maker account, so the agency went whole hog. The Hard Rock was theirs! Bonuses in pocket, everyone celebrated. Barry was sharing a joint with some of his guys when one of them pulled out a bag. He'd assumed it was cocaine. The guy called it Pure Serenity.

Whatever, Barry was willing. He could still rock out like a 25-year-old.

Cut to the trio doing lines in the bathroom.

Serenity came close to describing the warm rush that was a trademark of the opiate high. The opposite of cocaine, heroin wasn't so much about a kinetic buzz as it was the utter lack of one.

Barry had never felt that peaceful in all his life. Bliss so visceral, he could almost hear his brain letting go, dumping a lifetime of baggage, unshackling myriad constraints. Suddenly unencumbered, Barry was free...free to experience unmitigated joy, free to truly appreciate art, music, and even just breathing. Such was the mythology of the opiate.

Under its influence, there was never a sense of bliss ending or turning ugly. Heroin was total immersion. Hangover, Consequences, and Withdrawal might as well have been ghost towns.

Barry would never go there!

BARRY CAME TO and attempted a smile for the woman standing over him, who, he naturally assumed, was his wife. Groggily, he tried to sit up. Still in a fog, he played it cool. As far as he knew, Linda remained unaware of his drug habit.

"Hey Lin. I guess I was working too hard. We got a huge assignment at work and-"

"I am not your wife, Mr. Fine." The woman bent closer, revealing her face to him in the moonlight.

Barry tried to focus. Everything about the woman was undefined, vague.

Her opaque skin shimmered lustrously like mother of pearl. Her hair – long, white and fine – fell about her face and seemed to be moving. She appeared to be gowned in diaphanous material. The woman's features seemed too smooth, the curves of her body too subtle.

Regardless, she was not Barry's wife.

"I'm dead aren't I?" he asked. Or dreaming or hallucinating. Either way, he had to ask.

"You would be had She not intervened," the gowned woman answered.

"My wife?"

"Your God, Mr. Fine. The God of us all."

"Okay," Barry said, "I'm going to cover my eyes and when I remove the blanket you will be gone." Barry pulled the quilt over his eyes, but not before the cat got under there with him.

"You do not believe in God, I know. But tell me Mr. Fine. Do you believe in angels?"

"Not really," he mumbled from under the blanket. "I'm Jewish," he said, mustering a bit of sarcasm. "As a rule, Jews don't believe in angels. And seeing as you're not real anyway…"

"Actually, Mr. Fine," the gowned woman continued, "you have not been Jewish for most of your life. You certainly haven't conducted yourself as a Jew."

"The hell I haven't!" Barry barked. "I went to Hebrew school. A mohel circumcised me. Why am I arguing with a hallucination?"

The woman sighed. "Even though you had it printed in English, you botched the recitation at your bar mitzvah. Humiliated, you have never even tried to be religious."

Silence. Then from under the blanket: "How did you know that?"

"I already told you," she said. "I'm an angel."

The angel waved her arms releasing a flurry of tiny pixies! They flitted about the room like fireflies. Gathering over Barry, they descended, found the edges of his blanket, and lifted it up off of him. The fairies carried it across the room, draping it on Barry's writing chair. In vain, Sammy chased after them. With their tiny buzzing wings and glowing bodies, they looked like something from a Walt Disney movie.

"Jesus Christ!" Barry said, jaw dropping. He wasn't frightened. He was blown away.

"They're simple manifestations," the angel responded. She clapped her hands and, just like that, the pixies came together as one. They formed a glowing, swirling mass in the center of the room, which intensified, and in a flash, went out like a light bulb. They disappeared completely.

"Rather impressive, don't you think?"

Barry hadn't ruled out the last 15 minutes as pure hallucination. "I suppose I should be thankful they weren't pink elephants or hairy spiders."

"You should be thankful, period, Mr. Fine." The angel sat down on the couch beside him. With the edge of her sleeve she wiped his mouth of drool residue.

Barry let the woman mother him. Why shouldn't he? Her presence had to explain why he wasn't withdrawing or worse. He had no fever, no pain. He felt fine. Calm even. "Seriously," he asked. "Who are you?"

"Seriously. Your last chance."

Even if this angel was an apparition, she'd somehow provided him a reprieve from his anguish. He felt compelled to apologize, to confess. "I don't know how the drug thing got so out of hand," he said. "Usual story I guess. At first it makes you feel so good, then..." He laughed. "Wait a minute! Who am I talking to? Angels always feel good. Right?"

Even though it sounded glib, she gave his question serious consideration. "With us it's more the absence of feeling bad."

"That's how it is with heroin." Barry jumped in. "Not feeling anything bad at all."

"But we must *feel*," the angel sighed, showing frustration. She hadn't meant to advocate his drug use. Every minute on Earth she grew more human. Mistakes in judgment happened. "It is through suffering that we appreciate God's love."

"I thought God loved everyone. *Unconditionally.*"

Again, she felt her patience ebbing. "God has the capacity to love unconditionally. It's not a mandate." The angel cleared her throat. "While we know implicitly our family loves us, we must rely on faith that God does. Do you understand?"

Her analogy tripped Barry. "My family is not to blame for this," he rebutted. "They're what a man dreams about when he imagines having a wife and kid." He rubbed his forehead. "I honestly don't know how I let this happen." Barry kicked an empty Heineken bottle, sending it harmlessly sliding across the floor. They both observed the cat pawing after it.

"Your wife and child do love you, Mr. Fine. But sometimes we are not wholly sustained by another's love. It is a conundrum of the human condition. We crave love but when we are lucky enough to experience it we take it for granted. Once love is taken for granted it loses much of its power. I'm sorry but that's just the way it is. That is why faith in love is as important as love itself." The angel paused and took Barry's hand. "That is why I am here."

"You're here because you love me?" Barry contemplated the strange, glowing female sitting next to him. He had his doubts about her reality, let alone her intentions. Besides, she was starting to sound an awful lot like Dr. Phil.

"I don't love you, Barry. How could I? To say so would only cheapen the concept." She regarded his bloodshot, sunken eyes.

"You are working on something that can help us restore everyone's faith. Your life was spared because of your work."

Barry had to laugh. "As much as I appreciate the second chance, I write advertising for a living. It's mostly God-forsaken stuff. Trust me."

The angel approached Barry's desk. She picked up his laptop. "This is why I was sent here. This is why you are still alive."

"Sorry," Barry chuckled, "but you have me confused with another writer."

She forgave his inability to put two and two together. (Why do you think they called it dope?) "You are promoting goodness in all its forms, are you not?"

Keenly, Barry looked up. "You mean the Happy Soul Industry?"

"It is God's will."

"I'll be damned," exclaimed Barry.

"Apparently not."

Barry chewed his tongue. A nervous habit, it also proved he wasn't dreaming. What if these events were related, and divine? He played along. "I suppose God's agenda, if He has one-"

"She."

"If *She* has one..."

"Yes?"

"...would be to promote goodness in all of its forms."

"Bingo."

"And so the reason I'm not dead..." He pointed to the desk.

"That's right. You have work to do. The Lord's work." The angel wagged her index finger before him. "Think of it as atonement for those wasted bar mitzvah lessons."

"Be that as it may, our meeting is tomorrow," he said. "And guess what?" Barry pointed to the window. No longer pitch black, morning was imminent.

"Saving your life is but one of three miracles that will be performed here," said the angel.

"So you're going to help me write...be my muse so to speak?" He wasn't necessarily kidding. They were running out of time. He could use the help.

"Irma has already provided you ample inspiration. My gift to you will be your evening again."

"A do-over?"

She ignored his sarcasm, healthy in a writer. "Listen closely, Mr. Fine. You will have dinner with your girls, savoring every morsel. Then you will tuck your daughter into bed, reading her a story. You will kiss your wife goodnight, thanking her for being an extraordinary mother to your child. Then, and only then, you will adjourn to your office. *In that order.*"

She paused, making sure he got it. (The domestic details had not been part of God's plan. She'd put them in for good measure!) The angel finished her brief: "You then will have the whole of your evening to complete God's campaign."

"Wow. A fresh set of downs."

"The second miracle."

"Um, the only thing about that," Barry said, "is last night I was addicted to heroin and I'm pretty sure that when I wake up from whatever this is I will continue to be addicted to heroin."

"Think again." She grabbed his wrist, rotating it gently.

Barry raised his arm into the emerging daylight. He followed a familiar vein toward his elbow. He noticed right away: The needle marks were gone. He touched the skin and it was smooth. Come to think of it, his fingers weren't shaking. He had a miracle on his hands. Three of them, it seemed.

"You have work to do," said the angel. "And so I must bid you farewell. You will not remember me in the morning, Mr. Fine. But you will know... *better.*" The angel began to vibrate, her opaque figure fragmenting into pieces of light.

"Wait a minute," cried Barry. "What if I screw up? What if I can't do it? "

"Have faith in your higher power, Mr. Fine," she said, a swirl of colors now. "Use God!"

And then, like the twinkling remains of a firework, she disappeared.

"Easy for you to say," whispered Barry. He looked down. Sammy was rubbing up against his legs, mewing.

Was he hungry again? Thinking of food, Barry noticed the smell of baked garlic wafting into his office. Linda must be making spaghetti, he thought. It must be time for dinner.

SEVENTEEN

"How old are you, son?" Vernon asked, adding a smile. He doubted Luis was even twenty. They'd been in the car a half hour. Silence could be awkward. Vernon did not want it deadly.

"I'm not your son, Holmes," Luis shot back, derailing Vernon's 'happy talk' strategy.

Luis couldn't stand being called "son" by any man not his father, and his father was dead.

His father had abandoned the cane fields of Guatemala for a can factory in Oxnard.

His father was nothing like the well-dressed executive sitting next to him now.

He'd tried to succeed, his father had, or was that only the son's wishful thinking? When Papa lost half an arm in the automated presser, they'd sent him home with two months' severance and a case of Omaha Steaks. He pissed away the money and then the workers' comp on lottery tickets and cerveza. He was bitter, crippled, and drunk; and then he was dead.

Frustrated, Luis rapped his pistol on the dashboard. "Look, I didn't mean to go off just now," he said. "I'm having what you gringos call a bad day."

"Tell me about it," Vernon said. He flashed Luis the quickest of grins. It was not meant to provoke him, only an acknowledgement of the irony. Vernon had had few days as miserable as this one, to say nothing of the previous night.

A halfway decent student before dropping out of high school, yet Luis was unfamiliar with the concept of irony. Irony was for pretty, white folks. Where Luis came from, shit was shit and it happened all the time, irony free.

There was nothing ironic, for example, about his brother's arrest or the drive-by shooting that preceded it. He'd claimed ignorance his crew was carrying weapons. He'd only been along for the ride. One minute he's rolling a joint in the back seat and next thing he knew the windows were down and guns popping.

Of course, the police hadn't been interested in his brother's spin on things. So now he was doing time. And their Momma was back home crying. That wasn't irony, just bad luck and stupidity, part of being Latino and poor.

Luis changed the subject. "That's an expensive-looking suit, Holmes. Real nice."

"Name's Vernon. And you're right, Luis. This is a nice suit. And I've got at least a dozen more at home just like it." He wasn't bragging (under the circumstances that would be insane), he was just disclosing. It felt cathartic. He had no idea why.

"You can have a couple of them. I don't think they'd fit though. I'm a 44 long. You look more like a 42 regular. Am I right?"

"Either you high or you crazy." Luis didn't wait for a reply. Half the people he knew were one or the other. And *everybody* he knew talked shit. The Taco-Laco dog grinned down at them from a billboard. "That shit must be really pulling in money. I bet they love your ass at Taco-Laco."

"You'd think they loved my ass," laughed Vernon. "Same-store sales are up nearly 20 percent."

"Enough is never enough, eh Holmes?"

Traffic was thickening. They still had a way to go before Disneyland.

Vernon pulled into the carpool lane.

He mulled Luis's comment. Vernon concluded most everyone, on some level, realized wealth was in no way a precursor to happiness. Yet, most people (himself included) put the accrual of money on top of their list. As a business, Taco-Laco had to. But even with double-digit gains, they demanded more. "They want to capture customers for dinner," explained Vernon. "Taco-Laco owns lunch and late night but now they want the family hours as well."

"Shit, Holmes, I eat dinner there all the time. Fat Burger. Mickey D's. Until Wolfgang Puck can fill my gut for a fiver shit ain't ever going to change."

"You know who Wolfgang Puck is?"

"I know who he is but I never been to his place. I bet you have."

Maybe once, Vernon lied, adding that hardly anyone went to Spago anymore. He could tell that Luis wasn't buying it. After all, Puck was a celebrity. He'd been on television. Like Martha Stewart, his name had become a brand and a very marketable one at that.

"You're just dissing Wolfgang because he doesn't need to make commercials."

Luis' remark surprised Vernon, partly because of how telling it was. He took a deep breath. There was something chilling about a society where a human being cultivated an image in lieu of personality, a brand instead of a soul. Vernon thought of people like Michael Jordan, Tommy Hilfiger, Wolfgang Puck...and even Vernon Night.

"This is the XL, right?" Luis pointed his gun at the intricate control panel.

"Limited Edition XL." Vernon emphasized. Very hard machines

to get in Southern California, bidding wars were common. Vernon had two.

"Sweet," Luis whistled. "When you pull up in this people know you've arrived!"

Vernon faced his assailant. "And that's precisely what we've been telling the public: 'The Path Maker XL. It will move you and make you.'"

Luis brightened. "I'm all over those commercials, man! The one with CG in it? That's slick...I can't believe you make those, too."

"Neither can I," Vernon sighed. CG Cooper was the new superstar of the Los Angeles Lakers. Other than the job, he and Luis probably had a lot in common. Grew up in similar neighborhoods. Ran from the same kind of trouble. Ten inches and that many millions of dollars were all that differentiated the two. In a couple years CG Cooper was going to be a premier point guard in the National Basketball Association. Barring a miracle, Luis was going to be in jail or dead.

"Did you know CG doesn't read?" Vernon asked.

"Say what?"

"The man can't read, Luis. He's got millions of dollars in the bank but he can't write a check. Did you know that?" Vernon wasn't sure why he was telling Luis this. Was he trying to make a point? If so, what?

Luis jumped on him. "That's what an *entourage* is for, dude. You get a brother to watch your ass and a Jew to mind your cash. Sweeter than any book, baby!"

Vernon exhaled sadly, tapping the black leather steering wheel. He suddenly felt responsible for the negative events taking place not only in his life but in other persons' as well. Lord knew how many.

It will move you and *make you*.

No wonder Luis was drooling over a $77,000 truck. No wonder everyone did. His agency employed the best copywriters in America. Bandito Burritos. Limited Edition XLs. Whether a kid had five bucks in his pocket or five million, CN&W knew how to get it.

"Ads make people want things they don't need, Luis."

For the *Newsweek* article, he'd twisted the same words to mean something good. He knew it was true. But now he regretted it.

As they approached Disneyland, traffic thickened. Vernon slowed, falling into line. He observed two children making faces from the back seat of the car directly in front of them. One pulled a finger from his nose, pretending to flick boogers at them.

"I could waste him," said Luis, presumably joking.

Vernon shook his head. "No need, Luis. I'm sure the Disney Corporation will see to that."

If not irony, Luis got sarcasm. He shrugged, looking up the road, awaiting his first glimpse of the Magic Kingdom.

EIGHTEEN

With a screech, Evelyn wheeled her roadster into the last available parking space. A small lot, amidst a nondescript gathering of shops and businesses, it was hard to ignore the Asian woman bitching at them for taking her spot. Her car windows were up but David could tell she was pissed. The woman's arms flailed and her mouth moved irately. Meekly, he smiled back at the woman.

"Sorry about that," Evelyn said. "I didn't want to park this baby on the street." She checked her face in the rearview mirror and, finding some flaw, attended to it with a quick brush of mascara. "We're in a second-rate part of town."

"Second-rate?" The question was rhetorical. Still giddy from their latest round of lovemaking, for all David cared, they could be knocking on the gates of Hell.

"I suppose it's not that bad but it is where the people are. You know...*the real ones.*"

David played along. "Like our friend over there?" The Asian woman continued to glare at them from her double-parked car.

"Exactly," Evelyn said, snapping shut her compact. "A million bucks says she'll be in one of our groups."

"Won't that be awkward?" David grinned. "I mean, considering the scene she just made."

"We're separated from the groups by two-way glass. We can see them. They can't see us." She turned to him. "You've never been to a focus group before, have you?" When he didn't answer, she giggled. "A VP of marketing who's never done groups. That is *so* cute. I mean it."

Blushing, David felt compelled to explain. "Forgive me, Evelyn. I'm new at my post. I've...I should say we've...we've never needed to use focus groups before." Frustrated, he resorted to generalization. "At Happy Soul we do things differently!"

Evelyn countered: "For the most part, focus groups are a profound waste of time. But many of our clients demand them. Therefore, it's part of the process. Something we just do."

"Why?" David asked.

"Why are they a waste of time or why do we do them?"

"Both."

Evelyn smiled, patiently. In addition to being her lover he was a potential client. "The whole purpose of a focus group is getting an honest opinion about something we're doing or something we've done. We give consumers a few bucks and they give us a few thoughts. If something is right we figure out ways to exploit it. If something is wrong we either fix it or start over."

"That sounds reasonable," David said. "Even smart."

"On paper it's solid." Evelyn checked her watch. They were early. She'd give the Asian woman time to check in. Sure enough, she was crossing the street. "Problem is human beings don't behave honestly or naturally when they're being interrogated. They see the two-way mirrors. They know they're being observed."

"I should think the opposite would be true. Like in a courtroom. The whole truth and nothing but the truth." He wondered if focus groups were anything like the review committees God had spoken of, the ones that had spoiled the Garden of Eden.

Evelyn continued. "Big difference. We're asking for opinions, not facts. If you ask someone for an opinion, let alone pay them for it, they'll give it to you."

"But isn't that what you want?"

"Not necessarily. When you prod them to elaborate it creates dissonance, which corrupts the verbatim."

David tapped his chest. "New guy. Remember?"

"Look at it this way, when a commercial comes on in somebody's home a moderator doesn't follow with a series of questions and probes. In focus groups people are pressured to analyze material they might otherwise not." Evelyn paused, then added. "Commercials are not meant to be analyzed."

"Why would a person even want to participate? What does the average man care about an advertiser's agenda?"

"They don't. That's why we pay them." Evelyn had to laugh. "The average Joe doesn't give a damn what Madison Avenue has up its sleeve. And if he doesn't care you can bet an above-average Joe won't either!"

"So, who does attend? Who are these so-called *real people*?" David laughed nervously, amused, if not frightened, by the impromptu marketing lesson he was receiving.

"The unemployed. The lonely. Bored housewives. To some degree it depends on what kind of person we're looking for." Evelyn put on her sunglasses. "But it's safe to assume that whoever's in there actually needs the forty bucks."

"That doesn't sound like an ideal consumer."

"No it doesn't." Evelyn replied sharply. "Shall we see for ourselves?" She opened the car door.

Despite Evelyn's dreary explanation, David was excited. Even if focus groups were awful, he was with her. Smiling, he took her hand. "I'm sure we can get through them together." Arm in arm, they entered the complex.

People Systems had the weary, uncomfortable look of a dentist's office. Two administrators manned the reception desk, both very busy booking times and confirming appointments. Chairs rimmed every wall of two huge waiting rooms and most of them were occupied. Few, if any, seated participants were paired. Most read magazines or stared at their feet. Some ate. None talked. When Evelyn identified herself as a client, an escort promptly appeared.

They were separated from the waiting horde as quickly as possible, as if, David surmised, one group could corrupt the other. Quietly walking behind Evelyn, David did not require a focus group to point out her attributes. With each confident step she took, her silk slacks rippled, conforming to her body. He would follow her anywhere.

Before entering the small auditorium, the escort offered them food and beverages from a huge array outside the door. David took a bag of peanuts and Evelyn grabbed the Licorice Whips.

"Romantic, isn't it?" she observed, settling into their seats.

"I can't believe you were able to arrange all this on such short notice." David whispered.

"Nothing but the best for our clients," she said, squeezing his knee.

Alone in the theater, they faced a brightly lit conference room, which was filling up with participants. Right away, David noticed the Asian woman from the parking lot. She quickly took a seat, folding her hands. He counted seven other men and women.

To say folks were casually attired would be an understatement. One man wore shorts. Another had on sweats.

In comparison, the moderator, Edward, appeared downright professorial in bow tie and vest. But by his pallor, and downtrodden demeanor, it was obvious he'd been working in these caves for too long. Still, he was by far the most motivated of the group. Standing at the table's head, fiddling with his notes, he all but danced in anticipation.

"I think it's starting!" David exclaimed, a mouth full of peanuts.

"Okay, people," Edward began, "I'm going to begin with an odd question: How many of you perceive yourself to be a good person? Raise your hand if you do."

Two hands went up.

"Only two?" he asked. "I would have thought more."

"Good at what?" The question came from an older, bald man wearing sweatpants. His tee shirt depicted a scene from NASCAR.

"Good in general," answered the moderator. "Are you a nice person?"

"Well, I ain't ever been arrested."

"That is commendable," replied Edward. To himself he whispered: "Maybe even a little surprising."

"I not a bad person," the Asian woman said. She hadn't raised her hand but merely jumped in. "Bad people everywhere. I see all the time. Even in parking lot."

"Next time, please raise your hand," Edward said, politely. He kept smiling, having seen far worse than this lot.

David leaned over to Evelyn. "Everyone seems frustrated. Like caged animals."

"Not exactly a think tank is it?" Evelyn grimaced. She was determined to win David over. The focus group had limped out of its blocks, but maybe that made matters easier, giving them something to giggle about. "They probably came here expecting to talk about deodorant."

"They would not be seated at the Algonquin, if that's what you mean," quipped David in return. He'd actually met Dorothy Parker at a conference in New York and had enjoyed her wickedly smart presentation. He wondered if his reference had any meaning now. Evelyn *was* laughing.

"Let's play a game. Have some fun." Edward announced to the group. "I'm going to show you some pictures of well-known people. And I want you to tell me whether you think they're good people or bad people. If you think good raise your hand."

The Asian woman raised her hand.

"Indeed," Edward sighed. "But first I must show you the photo." Edward bit his lip. "That's easy enough, isn't it?" He wondered.

"Bad people everywhere," the Asian woman blurted again.

"Well if you see one then don't raise your hand. Now let's begin." He lifted the first placard, showing it to the room.

"That's Pete Rose!" David exclaimed. "He played for Cincinnati." David knew little of the modern world but he knew his Reds. He'd loved the team as a boy. And he still kept up with them now. He'd even met a few of the players in Heaven. God allowed the indulgence, even found it endearing.

"Wasn't he banned from the sport?" Evelyn asked. "For betting on his own team?"

"What are you saying?" Apparently, David did not know everything about his sports heroes. "Pete Rose...*banned*?" David got emotional, his voice higher. In his mind baseball epitomized everything that was great about America. Players weren't banned from anything, the Chicago Black Sox notwithstanding.

"Easy, Tiger," Evelyn said, soothingly. "They really can hear you."

David looked to see how the group would rule on the man they once called "Charlie Hustle."

"Okay," Edward said, squinting in the harsh light. "Only one person thinks Pete Rose is a good guy."

"Who Pete Rose?" the Asian woman demanded.

Moving on, Edward held up another card revealing a picture of Pope John Paul II.

A lanky man, sporting a Lion King tee shirt and dirty blue jeans, raised his hand forcefully. "Is this a joke? 'Cause that was the Pope! Wasn't nobody good as him." A large Hispanic man crossed himself, then raised his hand. Soon, everyone in the room had raised his or her hand.

"Okay," Edward asked, "Why is this person so good while the ballplayer is not?"

"He was the Pope!" the Latino man shot back. "The other guy... hell, he's just like the rest of us."

Before Edward could ask what he'd meant by "the rest of us," a pock-faced woman in her forties chimed: "If the Pope wasn't good then who is?"

"Anybody else?" Even Edward was surprised at how polarizing the two photographs were. He'd never done a group on a subject like this before.

As usual, however, Edward's personal opinion was diametrically opposed to the majority. He cared less about baseball and thought that the Pope had actually caused more harm than good. Birth control. Race relations. Gay rights. Here was a person that could change the course of human events with one speech. Why he'd steadfastly refused to alter the Church's antiquated dogma was heartbreaking and ultimately infuriating.

When Sinead O'Connor ripped apart his photograph on *Saturday Night Live*, Edward, for one, had cheered. "Let's simplify," he continued. "The Pope: good. Mr. Rose: bad."

"Well, if you put 'em one on one," remarked the fellow in sweats.

"There's beauty in this," Evelyn clucked. "Somewhere."

David leaned back, disoriented.

Baseball player bad. Pope good.

How could people be so complicated and simple-minded at the same time? So what if Pete Rose gambled. He knew for a fact that John Paul liked to play cards. Even God Herself enjoyed games of chance.

Then he remembered the devastated church from the television newscast. This world had its head screwed on backwards. Unscrewing it would be a daunting task.

The third photograph that Edward held up was of a former President of the United States. "Mr. William Jefferson Clinton," Edward announced. "Good guy? Bad guy?"

On either side of the mirror, a number of people laughed.

Dainty in her floral dress, an older black woman, Bernice, raised both hands. "I do believe he's both," she said.

Amused, Edward gestured for the woman to elaborate.

Bernice thought about it for a second. Figured everybody knew who the man was and what he'd done. No sense getting into that.

"It's like this," she said, really wanting to get her words right: "We put a boy from Arkansas in a position of esteem and power and then we surprised when he gets caught up by sin and depravity. Well, he was bound to slip. Bound to!"

She looked about the room and saw that she had an audience.

"No different with JFK. Great leader, God rest his soul. But he treated the office like a rooster in a henhouse!" She laughed loudly, and then took a big sip off her Orange Crush. "Good *and* bad. That's what I mean by both."

Which was easier, David wondered, turning around a bad person or a good person? Sadly, David feared the latter. He looked at his watch. His meeting with the other agency was in less than two hours. Grabbing a pen, he began scribbling notes.

Obviously, David was captivated. He clung to Bernice's every word. Having scored a direct hit, Evelyn decided to take advantage. "If you think this is good," she whispered in his ear, "come to New York with me. We'll really open your eyes."

David nodded. How could he not go?

In the conference room, Mr. Sweatpants argued that the wrestler, Stone Cold Steve Austin, had only turned evil temporarily. "Stone Cold joined the Forces of Darkness to fool the Undertaker. He's evil now. But when he opens that can of whupass...lookout bad guys!"

He then popped a handful of complimentary M&Ms into his mouth. "It's all good," he said, winking at Edward, who looked on, mortified.

NINETEEN

To accommodate his behemoth vehicle, Vernon pulled into a parking spot with no cars around it. It really made no difference; several years ago Disney had enlarged all the spaces, with sedans and station wagons going the way of merry-go-rounds and Ferris wheels. Vernon turned off the engine.

How to say it? They were never going to make it past the front gates, not with Luis carrying a gun. When it came to security, Disneyland had to be in league with the Pentagon. Thrilled by the revelation at first (Luis gets busted, game over), now he wasn't so sure.

What if Luis made a scene? They'd shared a lot during the surreal drive to Anaheim. Yet, carjacking aside, Luis didn't appear capable of hurting anyone. Vernon would take his chances in the car as opposed to near the crowded entrance. He knew that what he was about to say would challenge Luis, he just wasn't sure how.

"Let's do it, Holmes!" Luis said, forcing the issue.

Vernon took a deep breath. "You know, amigo, I could be wrong but they are probably not going to let you bring a gun into Disneyland."

At first the boy didn't respond. He looked at the gun. Then he closed his eyes. "Shit," was all he said, all he could say. He simply hadn't thought of that.

"I just realized it myself," offered Vernon. A variation on the Stockholm syndrome, Vernon actually felt sorry for his assailant.

Luis punched the glove compartment with his free hand. "Now what the hell am I going to do?"

Vernon pretended not to notice the lone tear as it rolled down Luis' cheek. "Well," he said tentatively, "you could leave the gun in the car."

Luis had a hard time trusting the people he knew, let alone a strange man, and under these circumstances. "Let me get this straight," he said. "You *want* to go to Disneyland?"

"Not really. But I will."

"And you won't run or call security?" Luis sniffled, wiping his wet cheek.

"You didn't shoot me."

Luis brightened. "But you don't even like Disneyland."

"You're right," Vernon said. "Frankly, I'd rather stick fondue forks in my eye than endure this pink and purple nightmare. But we're here."

"You're crazy, Holmes, but you're all right," replied Luis. He popped open the glove compartment and put the gun inside. "Let's do it!" Looking much like a father and son, the pair got out of the vehicle and headed toward the Magic Kingdom.

Not a weekend, Disneyland was less a mob scene, mostly school groups and Japanese tourists. Luis and Vernon made an odd couple but then so did Snow White and Goofy, the two characters who greeted them.

They decided to make their way up Main Street, USA.

Renovated many times, it was still essentially what Walt Disney had in mind: An iconic replica of a small, American town at the turn of the century, with candy shops, toy stores, and all kinds of eateries. Obviously, the tee shirt emporium wasn't vintage but one had to make room for concession.

"This doesn't look like the hood, that's for sure." Luis joked. "I mean where's the liquor store? The pawn shop?" Maybe he wouldn't admit it, but that was part of the reason he'd always wanted to come here, so he could experience an ideal neighborhood without being hassled by the cops.

"Make no mistake, Luis," Vernon said, "they've got other ways of taking your money."

Vernon had a theory about Disney. They were a lucrative cult that hid behind a cloak of wholesomeness. With endearing characters, popular movies, and an armada of toys, Disney hooked young people. And they got just as many as all the tobacco companies and spirits industries combined. First Junior sees the movie, and then he wants all the toys based on the movie. Then he sees the movie a second time. And finally, just when he's beginning to lose interest, they come out with the DVD and the cycle begins again!

What kid didn't know who the Little Mermaid was? What parent hadn't used Aladdin as a babysitter? Disney called it synergy but it was really an epidemic. What if Disney wielded that power for social or political reasons? What if they already were?

Vernon pointed to Buzz Lightyear, who happened to be strolling by. "To infinity and beyond. You know what that means, Luis?" Vernon asked, referring to the spaceman's popular catch phrase. "He's talking about all the money he's making!"

"So what?" Luis said. "He's just doing his job."

A bunch of children ran by them as if chasing a ball. A frazzled woman struggled to keep up, probably their teacher. It was going to be a long day.

"I'm just saying it's creepy," cited Vernon. "A cartoon character making all this money off a bunch of kids."

Luis didn't even have to think about it. "Your Taco-Laco dog does the same thing, Holmes. Makes money off of kids."

Wow. Vernon had to stop. He thought about all the dinner parties he'd nearly ruined espousing his evil Disney theory. His point of view had remained unchallenged, up until now, and from all people, an impoverished teenager. Before he could reply Luis hopped on one of the theme park's ubiquitous omnibuses. Vernon ran to catch up.

"Get with the program, Holmes!" Luis shouted. He'd scrambled to the upper deck, Vernon huffing after.

"Where are we going?" Vernon asked, settling beside him.

"Space Mountain."

"Space Mountain. Is that still here?" Vernon remembered the ride from his own childhood, an all-enclosed roller coaster, the world's first.

"They added electricity since you been on it," Luis said, sarcastically.

"Wise ass."

"Takes one to know one." They rode in silence, but it was far from quiet. Disneyland was not famous for beatific quietude. On their right a parade passed. On their left gymnasts completed a routine. On both sides, children were going nuts. Everything was beckoning and yet intimidating. The place dared you from every corner.

"I had a job like yours." Luis was sincere.

"Oh really?" Vernon was too.

"Tagging for clubs. Hyping music." Luis elaborated. "We made posters for our *peoples* in the hood. They paid us to make them and they paid us to put them up. Got pretty good at doing both."

"You mean like stapling flyers on a telephone pole?" Vernon had an idea he was wrong.

"Hell no!" Luis said, confirming Vernon's hunch. "This wasn't 'Have-You-Seen-My-Dog.' Our shit was dope." Even provoked, Luis kept his voice down, sensitive to all the children.

"So were you the artist or the writer?"

"My brother drew but I did most of the thinking."

"Make any money?" Vernon really wanted to know.

"We broke even on materials," answered Luis. "The green came from executing the run."

Lost, Vernon shook his head. "Executing the run?"

"Holmes, we covered our territory proper," Luis explained. "Telephone poles are for amateurs. I got my clients on buses, walls, and windows. We took over the hood. By the time you woke up on Saturday our stuff was everywhere."

"Isn't that illegal?" Vernon asked, knowing full well it was. Still, these so-called wild posters were among the latest weapons in urban marketing. Chloe Night used them where appropriate, whenever possible. But *executing the run* was difficult; there were few places one could legally "tag."

"We broke the law. Then you learn where you can bend it. You figure out who's your friend. But now with my brother out of circulation..."

The omnibus entered another realm, all silver towers and rockets, a monorail cutting through overhead. A dated vision of the future, tomorrow never turned out as fantastic as predicted, the new millennium bringing only a rash of new headaches and "Best of Century" lists. But the fantasy remained on this patch of land in Anaheim.

"What do you suppose the future holds?" Vernon asked.

"For me..." Luis replied, solemnly. "*Nada.*"

Even rhetorically, it was a foolish question. Had Vernon forgot whom he was with and the unusual context of their visit? "I'm sorry about your brother," Vernon said, making amends. "I'm sure you wish he was here."

"We had a lot of plans but what can I do?" Luis shrugged in the way that teenaged boys do. "After a while it's easier if you just stop making plans."

"Funny, I just gave a speech about planning..."

Vernon flashed on all that had happened to him recently, the series of unfortunate events and frustrations. Had any of that been planned? Would it have made the slightest difference? Vernon had an epiphany: All that had happened to him was nothing compared to what Luis was going through. For the first time in a long time he actually felt compassion for someone other than himself.

"Maybe we don't need planners, per se," he mused. "But we all need plans."

A father got on board the omnibus with his two sons, both boys not much younger than Luis. The youngsters were wearing the green and gold jerseys of Green Bay's storied football team. Dad was videotaping everything. Obviously tourists, they were having a grand time.

Vernon doubted Luis had ever attended a professional football game, let alone with his father.

Did a father even lay claim to him? He'd lost a brother.

The rules were posted at the entrance to Space Mountain: You had to be at least this tall. No one could get on wearing a pacemaker. Other things, as much for show, as it was good advice. They did nothing to hamper anyone's excitement. Nor did the excessive queue. Good things come to those who wait!

And it was right then and there that Vernon decided to do something good with his life. "Luis, I've been thinking..."

"You're not chickening out are you?"

"Actually, it's more of a proposition."

Luis looked at him nervously. He'd been *propositioned* before.

Vernon smiled. "I want you to come work for me, Luis. I want to give you a job."

Observing the families around him, Luis fantasized what it would be like to be part of something, part of something real. He'd known unity before, but mostly from gangs, which he now struggled to avoid. He and his brother had been a team. Luis wanted to feel that way again. But this couldn't be *that*, could it?

Ahead of them in line, two youngsters squealed, swinging from their daddy's arm. Blissfully content, their happiness was a given.

"For real?" Luis replied. Bursting inside, he tried to maintain his composure. "I don't even own a suit."

"Nobody in advertising does." Vernon beamed. "I want you to teach my team how to *execute the run*."

Even as he said the words, Vernon knew it was the right move: A brilliant idea for his company and a life-changing event for this boy. Unlike pro-bono work, this act of kindness was free from ulterior motive.

Vernon had himself a win-win.

"You'll pay me a salary? I get a 401K?" In his mind Luis had taken the job, but he wanted a minute to think.

No stranger to negotiation, Vernon did not mind the question. He answered it with another: "What was your best week when you were hanging posters with your brother?"

"We could make a thousand dollars," Luis responded, telling the truth.

Vernon added it up quickly. "That's about 52 grand a year. I tell you what...I'll give you 60 thousand."

A gaggle of Japanese girls moved up in the line, all wearing the same tight spandex and concert tee shirts.

Luis preened, fixing his hair. One or two smiled at him, giggling nervously. He waved, prompting more reaction. Luis imagined himself as a high-flying executive. How impressed would they be then? More profoundly, he envisioned his mother, her tears over his brother turning to those of joy over him.

Oblivious to the flirting, Vernon continued. "It's called urban marketing. And you can be our guru! I'd like for you to attend a meeting tomorrow." The wheels turned faster as he warmed to his subject.

"Hey Holmes, first things first!"

Luis pointed to the dark entrance of Space Mountain looming ahead of them. As excited as he was about the job, this was still Disneyland's premier attraction and Luis was, after all, only a teenager.

"Just tell me we have a deal," Vernon insisted, focusing on the bigger journey. He held out his hand.

"I'll have to get back to you." Luis waited a beat.

"Of course we have a deal, Holmes!"

Instead of shaking hands, the young man embraced Vernon in a full-on hug. He said it again: "You're crazy, Holmes...But you're all right!"

Vernon had to agree with him, on both counts, the latter making the former a hell of a lot easier to manage.

TWENTY

"**O**KAY, what shall we read this evening?" Barry asked his baby girl. He thumbed through her basket of books, not recognizing many of the titles. Had it been that long since he'd read her a story? "What happened to *The Very Busy Spider*?" He recalled it as being one of her favorites. His anyway.

"Oh Daddy," Jessica admonished, "We don't read that one anymore. It's for *babies.*"

"I see," he replied. "And I suppose we've graduated from *The Little Red Hen* as well?" Having been inattentive to his daughter for months, if not years, he had no clue what she was capable of reading.

"Make up a story, Daddy!" Jessica demanded. She sat up in bed, crossing her arms. In the lamplight, Barry could see she had her mother's auburn hair, though more curly like his own, and already a spray of freckles. It was as if he was looking at his daughter for the very first time...

Just before she was born, Barry went on a lengthy television shoot in London. When he eventually returned, after almost two months, he couldn't believe how much his wife had changed. With her swollen belly, new haircut, and maternity clothes, she looked completely different from the woman he'd gotten pregnant. Back then he had an excuse for his absences. Production could devour so much of a copywriter's time (even more so for art directors). But addiction to drugs was far more insidious a mortgage, because even at home he wasn't really there.

Humbled by the chance to reclaim fatherhood, Barry could not take his eyes off of the beautiful child sitting atop her bed. *His beautiful child.* Ironically, he was so smitten he'd forgotten what they were talking about! No matter: They were talking. That's what counted. Unable to stifle his emotions, Barry hugged his daughter. "You're very special to me," he said, his voice breaking. "I just want you to know that."

"I believe you, Daddy," Jessica replied, "but you still have to tell me a story. A made-up one, not from the book basket!" Her daddy was acting funny and he needed constant reminding.

"I don't know. It's been a while," he said, pulling away from her gently. He discreetly wiped the wetness from his cheek.

"You're a writer, aren't you, Daddy?"

"Well, yes, I suppose..."

"Writers make up stories, don't they?" She nodded, as if to say, see, that's all there is to it!

Jessica had a point. If he could write the words that convinced people to pay hundreds of dollars for a pair of sneakers, he should be able to conjure up a bedtime story for his daughter.

"Once upon a time..." he said, pausing, fumbling for inspiration.

Jessica flopped backwards onto her big pillow. Even though everybody started stories that way she didn't find it offensive. On the contrary, she relished that her father was responding to the challenge and, more importantly, was grateful for his attention. He'd been conspicuously absent from her life for what seemed like an eternity and she wasn't about to let him off the hook. She slipped under the covers, tucking herself in.

Barry continued. "There once was a pretty blue bird who was looking for a juicy worm to eat. The bird searched under every stone and turned over every leaf. But she could not find a single worm and she was getting very, very hungry."

"Ewwwie!" Jessica squealed, turning her face into the big pillow. "I hate worms!"

"But not the blue bird," Barry exclaimed. "She loved worms. 'Why can't I find a squiggly-wiggly worm to eat?' she asked her friend the purple-spotted salamander, who lounged nearby on a rock.

"The salamander replied: 'Why not just eat the seeds scattered on the ground?'

"The blue bird was saddened by the amphibian's words. 'But I want a worm to eat,' she said. 'Worms are what I *always* eat.'" Barry made a sad face to accentuate the blue bird's predicament. But his frown was sincere, for in a way, the blue bird's desperate longing mirrored his own. He pressed on.

"The salamander considered the blue bird's quest to find a worm. He'd had worms to eat before. They were okay but certainly not better than seeds. He shrugged, bewildered by the bird's pointless craving. 'You want what you cannot have while ignoring the perfectly good food all around you.' The salamander sighed when he spoke, feeling sorry for his pretty but silly friend. 'I'm afraid,' he whispered, 'for this reason, you will never be happy.'

"'I don't understand,' the blue bird chirped in dismay. 'A fat worm is what I have always dreamed of. It is what all blue birds dream of.'"

"Poor, sad blue bird," Jessica clucked, shaking her head. "Why can't she be content? She has seeds to eat and a caring friend. Lots of people don't have either. What's her problem?"

Barry was enthralled by his daughter's involvement in the story, as well as in her wise opinion. Content was a big word and she'd used it correctly. It was an even bigger idea. Barry didn't know where the story was going but he realized where it had come from. The blue bird was speaking from *his* heart. It wanted sustenance.

"What's her problem? The salamander thought the very same thing. 'There is so much to enjoy and it's right in front of you!' He preached to the bird. 'Why do you obsess on what you cannot have?'

"'Because that is what we pretty birds do. It's in our nature,' the blue bird said, confounded. 'Why do you think we always have our beaks to the ground?'

"'Do you see this flower?' asked the purple spotted salamander.

"The blue bird said, 'Of course I see that flower. How could I not? It is far too lovely to have been missed.'

"'Well,' the salamander replied. 'That lovely flower came from the same, simple seeds you choose to ignore. Just as you came from a simple boring egg.'

"The blue bird nodded quietly. She admired her shimmering blue feathers and thought about the dull egg she'd emerged from a long time ago. Could it be that the salamander was right? She thought about things for a while.

"'I have to get off this rock,' the salamander said. 'The sun is getting hot on my skin. But heed my words: Enjoy what God has provided for you and be thankful She has provided anything at all.' With that the salamander crawled off his rock and slithered into a cool spot under the log. Salamanders love logs."

"You said 'She,' Daddy!" Jessica interrupted. "Everybody knows that God is a man."

Barry opened his eyes. (He'd been telling the story with both of them closed.) "Did I really? Maybe I was thinking of the blue bird. Or even you!"

"Silly Daddy! Finish the story now. Does the bird finally eat the seeds? Or does she keep looking for worms?"

"Let's see," Barry said. "The blue bird plucked one of the shiny, black nuts off of the ground. She rolled it around in her beak. Thought about spitting it out. But didn't! Thought about it some more..."

"Daddy!" Jessica threw a stuffed animal at him. "Stop teasing!"

"The blue bird bit into the seed," he said. "And then…" Barry rushed over to his daughter and bit her on the tummy. "Chomp! Chomp! Chomp!"

Jessica howled, writhing delightfully in her father's arms. She begged him to stop tickling her but, of course, when he did she wanted him to do it some more!

Instead, Barry elected to finish his story.

"The blue bird began eating all the seeds and she enjoyed them, too. 'I had no idea how good these were!' the blue bird exclaimed. From a distance, the salamander observed his friend and shook his purple, bumpy head. He knew all along!

"'The truth of the matter is,' the blue bird said, 'I pretended not to like the seeds because deep down I wanted something better.' The blue bird hung her head in shame.

"The salamander beamed. 'Then don't be sad. Rejoice instead! Just because a thing was never lost doesn't mean you can't enjoy finding it again.' He slithered deeper into the large, mushy log he called home. 'I must leave you now,' he said to the blue bird, 'but you've learned a great and valuable lesson.' The salamander flicked his slimy tail and departed from view.

"And from that day forward," Barry said, "the blue bird never wanted for anything again because now she appreciated everything she had. And, guess what? No surprise here. She lived happily ever after."

"Is she the Blue Bird of Happiness, Daddy?"

Barry smiled at his bright child. Even he, the master of puns, hadn't seen that one coming. "Well, Jes, I suppose she is. And do you what that makes you?"

"What?" Jessica said, giggling in anticipation.

"That makes you the squiggly-wiggly worm!" He grabbed his daughter and began tickling her again. He held on tightly, thinking he might not ever let go.

TWENTY-ONE

UNPREPARED as she was, Mila fretted. Everyone should be fretting. Their big meeting was less than an hour away and the food still hadn't been delivered. Who was setting up the computer for projections? Because Mila did not do technology! And where were Vernon and David anyway? Couldn't have this meeting without them.

Forgetting her mantra, Mila began reciting the Serenity Prayer. She ran the portable vacuum over the boardroom table; even that hadn't been cleaned properly. Still smarting from the Eye Job, she couldn't see whether she was actually picking up any debris. Her frustration mounted.

Integral to the Humanologist's creed was remaining calm and collected. Having achieved Clarity, she should have had less difficulty maintaining her composure. But it was exceedingly trying considering the client – correction, *potential* client – had been waiting in the lobby for 25 minutes!

PATIENTLY, DAVID PERUSED the framed print ads mounted on the wall outside the main conference room. Having too much nervous energy to actually concentrate on them, he flitted from one to the other like a honeybee.

Light traffic, coupled with his eagerness, meant he'd arrived for the meeting painfully early. David pursed his upper lip, enabling another tantalizing hint of his lover's scent. She was still on his lips, on his mind.

Oddly, thinking of Evelyn helped calm his nerves over the imminent pitch. In the insurance business he'd done his share of presentations and the first few had been traumatizing. He'd stammered and sweated and hated every second. But, with repetition, eventually they'd become routine – a good thing, seeing as management expected every salesman to give the same speech, over and over again. Getting through it correctly was as important as making a sale. Subsequently, no one at the company had skills in public speaking. Few people in America did. At the time, personal style was considered irrelevant to doing a good job, if not inappropriate. Business in general was played close to the vest, hence the creation of the phrase itself. In the late nineteenth, early twentieth century, if one wanted to see a show, one went to the circus.

Times do change. David marveled at how cleverly each ad on the wall handled its selling proposition, some couching the message, others flaunting it. He could only imagine the flamboyance of their creators.

Other than the occasional salesman who'd shown up at his door (selling brushes, elixirs, or sweepers), David had never been pitched a day in his life. Despite his preparation, and even God's counseling, he still wasn't sure how to play the role. What if he didn't like something? What if he had to say no?

The many agency luminaries who'd convened in Heaven all bitched (to the degree that one bitched in Heaven) about "the client from Hell." While not wanting to be a pushover, David had no interest in being "the client from Hell."

"You're such an angel for waiting, Mr. Angelo," Mila greeted him, a cup of coffee in one hand and a bottle of water in the other. "I didn't know which one you'd prefer..."

He accepted the water graciously. With his ever more human nerves jangling, the last thing he needed was a cup of coffee.

David opened the plastic bottle, taking a sip. As it had at the focus group and elsewhere, the water tasted exactly like...water! Madly curious as to why H_2O came in bottles, he'd also noticed that every person in Los Angeles seemed to drink from them. He was afraid of asking why and being perceived as naïve.

The young woman stood before him, smiling yet quiet. She seemed pensive. David assumed it was because the agency's principals had not been present to greet him. But he'd come early and, in fact, the men were only a few minutes late. He drank his water and smiled back at Mila, wishing he could reassure her that all was just fine. "Will you sit with me for a moment?" David motioned to the small sofa nearby.

"I can do that," Mila replied, sitting down beside the gentleman.

Feeling brave – or just nervous – she initiated the conversation. "So, Mr. Angelo, are you married?"

She wasn't flirting. Far from it. She was merely trying to make a potential client comfortable.

Unfortunately, it had the opposite effect and David was taken aback by her query. He did not want to tell her that his wife was long dead. But lying continued to be a rotten alternative. He stammered. Now they both were uptight.

Mila knew she'd misspoken. "My gosh, I'm so sorry!" She could tell right away by the look on his face. "I just noticed that you don't have no ring and, well, I know it's none of my business..."

Don't have no ring?

She knew better than to speak like that. She hated ad-libbing, not having a script; it made her nervous, causing her to slip. Had she forgotten her Humanology dicta? *Professional conversation was dialogue. It could be memorized and rehearsed.* Her swollen eyes ached from yesterday's hard "lesson" and she yearned to rub them.

Seeing Mila in pain, and recognizing that she was only trying to please him, David gently patted her hand. "That's quite all right. I need to be able to answer that question anyway." David sighed. "You see, my wife passed away some time ago."

"I'm sorry," Mila apologized again. And she was sorry. But she was also mad at herself. *Never ask a question unless you know the answer.* She'd learned that one a long time ago, in maybe her first session at the Church. Simple questions could have complicated answers. For example: *How are you?*

While not her guardian angel, surely there was something David could do to make this woman feel better. If only he knew her better.

From their conversation he'd gleaned a bit. He intuited that Mila regarded people as either greater than or less than herself, above or beneath her in status. For whatever group she was in, she probably created a caste system, putting herself on a lower tier. David supposed that as a prospective client he was put near the top.

Compelled to remove himself from that pedestal, David launched right in. "May I ask you a personal question, Mila?"

The tactic worked. Mila loosened up, smiling again. "Oh would you? That would make me feel so much better. Ask anything!"

"Your eyes," David said, pointing to his own. "Have you been crying?"

He, of course, referred to the scarring she'd gotten from the *Eye Job.* Odd, he'd likened it to crying. But very astute of him. For she had been crying. Supposedly "clear" now, the ballyhooed confidence alleged to come with advanced auditing hadn't. If anything, she'd been feeling worse the last few days, more foolish and insecure than ever.

"I have been crying, Mr. Angelo. But that's not why my eyes are this way." Mila sighed.

"I suppose it would be easier if I said I had some work done, which, in a way, I did." She paused, trying to think of the correct words. "I'm just not supposed to talk about it."

From the way she rode up on her sentence David got the idea she would. "I see," was all he needed to say.

"Well, actually, I'm the one who's supposed to be seeing," she said, pouncing on his timely choice of words. "Clearer than ever, according to the Church."

The angel startled. He had not expected her to bring up a church. Obviously familiar with many religions, David was unaware of any that had a procedure involving one's eyes. He wondered, though doubtfully, if Mila referred to some form of stigmata.

Regardless, she'd certainly piqued his curiosity. "What faith are you," he queried, "if you don't mind me asking?"

"I was born Catholic..." She fingered a rivulet of her flowing, black hair. "But that's not the church I'm talking about." She forced a laugh. "They're not anything alike. Trust me! They...I mean we... we don't believe in God like that."

Mila looked this way and that. Opening up was a violation of the rules. Nevertheless, she continued. "We believe that God is like this vast potential stored inside us. We are all connected to it by an ancient alien society. Individuals can achieve anything they want by tapping into this shared energy."

Alarmed, David did not have any idea what Mila was talking about. He seriously speculated on whether she did as well. "With all due respect, Mila, you pray to extra- terrestrials?"

"It's more about personal actualization. We pretty much skip over the stuff about space men. After all, it's called Humanology." Mila remembered having had a similar reaction to the alien component. But that was a year ago, maybe longer. Somehow, she'd gotten over or around it; everyone in Hollywood had.

Cults were not unknown to David but he'd never heard of Humanology. He wondered about God's take. With few exceptions, She viewed cults the same way most citizens did: Warily. Her primary worry was for the safety of individuals, rather than the integrity of these groups.

Still, David remained a gentleman, and an angel. Even though concerned, he played it cool. "Can you talk about your eyes?"

She was nervous about discussing the Church's business, yet he couldn't help but notice her tension subsiding with each revelation. "My eyes were held open with a device so that I could see...so that I might achieve Clarity. The process hurt." Carefully, she touched the bruised flesh located around her eye sockets. "It still does."

Once again, appalled. Once again, David showed restraint. "That does sound painful."

"I know what it sounds like," cried Mila. "It sounds crazy."

David took both Mila's hands in his.

"God *is* within us all, Mila. And personal growth *is* directly related to how we connect with God. But there is no map on how to get there. No course we can audit. No syllabus." He laughed, but warmly. "If it worked that way your pitch today wouldn't be necessary, now would it?"

Mila looked down, unable to meet his eyes. Compared to her parents' criticism of Humanology, David's reprisal came lovingly. It also reminded her why he was at the agency.

She had to ask: "Is the Happy Soul Industry a church?"

"We represent goodness, be it derived from conventional religions or elsewhere. In that regard, even your church qualifies. But remember, while pain is part of any spiritual journey we don't advocate putting people through it. It's not about tests and regulations, or even achievement."

Mila had the unfortunate revelation that maybe she'd wasted an awful lot of time and money. Still, she fought him half-heartedly; the way a child does when caught in a lie. "What about the Bible? It has rules and regulations."

"Way too many," agreed David. He recalled his earlier conversation with God, in the old temple. "But that's why so few people read the darn thing, let alone abide by it."

"Lots of people still read the Bible," Mila responded. Her mother did, night after night, often to her... from the phone!

"Old ladies and priests," David sighed. "We need to reach people who are more easily distracted." He punctuated the thought. "We need to make goodness cool. That's the number one reason I'm here."

"I'm glad to hear you say that, Mr. Angelo." Vernon said, sauntering over. He had on corduroy dress slacks and a Polo shirt. His blazer slung over his shoulder. This was casual for Vernon, highly casual, considering the agenda.

Mila's wounded eyes widened at the sight of a young Latino by his side. She ogled the pair. Full of surprises, Vernon promptly gave Mila a big hug.

"You on some new medication, Vern?" But her smile was as big as his.

Ignoring the remark, he turned to David. "It's a big day....What do you say we get to it?"

Humming, Vernon ushered them across the foyer, opening the fancy metal doors that led to the main conference room.

Entering into sunshine, they viewed a striking oval surrounded by windows, some with balconies and potted palms. On the center table was a delightful spread of fruit and other tropical treats. The food had come! Barry and Irma were waiting. They had on Ray-Ban sunglasses.

Vernon spoke, his voice booming: "Of course, you remember the creative engine at Chloe Night. My partner, Barry Fine."

Taken aback by Vernon's flattering introduction, Barry almost lost his train of thought. He handed David a pair of the iconic sunglasses.

"Hopefully, our work is so bright you'll need them!" Not waiting for laughs, "Anyway, this is my creative partner, Irma."

"How are you, sir?" Irma smiled politely as David adjusted the glasses to his nose.

"And now," Vernon beamed, "I'd like you to meet our agency's newest member. Luis brings an expertise in urban marketing, which will really help us in those tough, cynical markets."

"Hello, Luis," David said, extending his hand. "I'm glad to meet you." And he was. Luis was the first teenager David had met since returning to Earth. For God's agenda to be fulfilled he felt they were going to have to meet a whole lot more.

"Hey, how's it going?" Luis nearly shouted, vigorously shaking the angel's hand.

"Luis has a lot of passion," Vernon said. "HSI will need to reach people just like him and Luis can help show us how to do it."

"Splendid," David replied. He liked the energy surrounding these two. Indeed, it was like it had followed them in the room. Vernon seemed more enthusiastic than the last time they'd met. Angels could detect karma, and David was getting high readings from Night and his young associate, from all of them, really.

Mila coughed, probably by design.

"Where are my manners?" Vernon smiled. "Luis, I'd like you to meet my secretary and right-hand man, Mila Rodriguez."

Mila extended her hand.

"She may be your secretary, Mr. Night, but in no way is she a man!" He kissed Mila's ring finger. "Buenos dias, Ms. Rodriguez."

"Hola," Mila replied, incredulous. Normally, the last exchange would have offended her, especially in front of a new client, but this morning contained too many surprises to get hung up in semantics. Besides, Luis was just like every boy she'd grown up with in the neighborhood. Coming down on him would be like incriminating a brother. And since when did she rely on protocol anyway? The good vibes emanating from them had not escaped her either.

"Ahem!" Vernon got everyone's attention. "Today is a great day and we're going to keep it that way. That means no PowerPoint. No eye charts. Let's just talk about ideas. One idea in particular..."

As he spoke, the small group seated themselves, save for Barry, who made his way to the front of the table.

The presentation began.

"How are you?" Barry asked, getting things rolling. "It's a simple question, isn't it? Small talk. We just used the phrase on each other moments ago. We use it all the time. Typically, the corresponding answer we give is 'Fine.' As in 'I'm fine. How are you?'"

Barry paused, for effect.

"But are we fine? What if we had to really answer the question? What if we had to answer the question from the depths of our souls?"

At this point, Irma stood, revealing a placard with the phrase written upon it: **How Are You?** She'd chosen a classic typeface, Helvetica, set in black against white with just a hint of drop shadow.

Barry resumed his patter. "What if we compelled people to answer the question? What if we could make 'How are you?' a clarion call to society? What if Happy Soul Industry asked society the question and really wanted an answer…the real answer? What if Happy Soul could initiate meaningful dialogue with consumers by virtue of asking this one simple question?"

Barry grasped Irma's sign. Holding it aloft, he circled the table, not unlike a boxing ring girl between rounds. Excitedly, he continued: "David, if we do this right, the most popular question in the world will become the most important question in the world…and it's being asked by the Happy Soul Industry!"

Barry let his audience absorb the concept.

"How… are… you?" He emphasized each word. "Not so small a question now, is it?"

And so the discussion went from three simple words to a far bigger proposition. Irma showed David the transit cards, the billboards, and the newspaper ads. David got and appreciated how the agency had linked its message with specific media, talking to waiting pedestrians for instance. Barry read several strong radio scripts, in which people actually did answer the question, honestly and from their hearts. At an appropriate moment, Vernon assured David they could deliver this clarion call to even the meanest of streets. Luis gamely explained to him the concept of tagging; showing examples he and his brother had done for an underground record label.

From start to finish, it was a well-honed and engaging presentation. So much so, Mila actually applauded. No one besmirched her for the indiscretion.

And certainly not David, for whom the idea revealed its simple genius early on; the broad smile that appeared on his face never left.

"God, you're going to love this," David whispered, as he stared at all the propaganda in the room. As he spoke to God all the time, the comment just slipped out.

"Excuse me?" Vernon asked, fishing for more positive reinforcement. Had he heard the man correctly?

Unafraid to be heard, the angel laughed, and raised his voice: "I said, God I love this!" He then gave everyone in the room a standing ovation.

TWENTY-TWO

ON the Red Eye to New York, the cabin was quiet and dim. Evelyn dozed as David thumbed through a magazine. He occupied the window seat and she the other two, her head leaning on his shoulder. Behind them an older couple played cards.

They had leveled off some time ago, smoothly soaring at 37,000 feet, when David heard a woman calling his name. At least he thought he'd heard a woman's voice. And something about it was very familiar.

He turned toward Evelyn. Even while she slept, he couldn't help but admire her stunning profile. His eyes inevitably wandered to the alluring, ominous tattoo, just visible above the waistline of her skirt. It made his heart skip, and other organs as well. Evelyn murmured but she was still very much asleep. It hadn't been she who'd addressed him. So who?

David discreetly looked over his shoulder, over the seat cushion.

The elderly couple stared right back at him; their big glasses seemed to shine in the darkened cabin, making them look like raccoons.

Embarrassed, David mumbled something about looking for his pillow and turned around. He directed his gaze to the blackened portal.

Cheekily, God waved to him. Sitting on the plane's wing, the rushing atmosphere broke around her like white smoke, her luminous hair whipping in the wind as a tail would on a comet.

"My God!" David nearly screamed, somehow holding his tongue.

As a knee-jerk reaction, he slammed the window blind shut.

Meaning no disrespect, he quickly reopened the blind, where he observed God, oblivious to the elements, essentially surfing upon the wing's frame! She appeared to be enjoying herself.

David panicked, but managed to whisper, "Dear Lord, what if someone sees you?"

"I suppose," she chortled, "they won't believe their eyes!"

That did not make him feel better. "What are you doing here? Or should I say *there*?"

God had no trouble understanding him. The loudly humming engines were no impediment either; if anything, they masked their voices from everyone else's, affording them some privacy.

"As for your question," replied God, "I can't very well sit down beside you." She did not have to point to Evelyn.

"Should I be jealous, David?"

"Dear God no!" he blurted, suddenly very embarrassed.

What did She know? What did She think? He'd not only taken a lover but now he was going to New York to solicit an advertising agency, the latter being something God had specifically suggested they not do. Who knew how She felt about the former?

"Are you displeased…with me?" He had to ask.

"Of course not." God smiled, walking along the wing toward David. The intense velocity thrust upon Her was having only a cosmetic effect. God's long hair shimmered behind Her, the comet's tail getting brighter. She came right up to his window.

"Although, I should warn you: you and yours might find the Rocky

Mountains a bit turbulent this evening!" She winked at him, giving the window a kiss.

David knew his was not a vengeful God, but still.... "I'm sorry I have taken various liberties, my Lord. Can you forgive me?" He assumed She knew everything.

"Forgive you? For what?" God became serious. "You must remember, David, I empowered you to do whatever you felt was necessary for the Happy Soul Industry. And for yourself. Maybe you're confusing liberties with opportunities."

The plane hit an air pocket, causing them to dip. God bounced up and away from the wing, but quickly resumed Her place.

"I told you," she said. "Turbulence! But don't you see? Your actions are no more or less surprising to me than a moment of wind shear. I did not see the bump coming any more than I knew what you would do on your return to Earth. I don't hold all the cards, David. I react to things. Same as you."

David relaxed. Like the white noise coming off the airplane engines, God's comment was soothing.

"She's lovely, David," God said, changing the subject. "Do you trust her?"

"Trust? Why do you choose that word, my Lord? Over all others?"

"You mean in lieu of love?"

David glanced at Evelyn. She was still sleeping. "Yes. Why not 'love' or even 'like?'"

"Trust is more critical here."

"I thought love-"

"Perhaps it is more important...for mortals."

David sighed, realizing what She meant. This mission would end. His time on Earth was limited. Given that reality, trust was more relevant.

"In a way they are both the same," She said, softening. "But of this I am certain: One can fall in love overnight. The development of trust may take a lifetime."

Melancholy overcame David. The concept of God was so inextricably linked with love that he had a hard time separating the two. "God is Love" was written above the altar at his childhood church.

"Do you have a dollar bill?" God asked.

David looked at Her blankly. He hadn't really thought about hard currency. He didn't have to. Not when he'd been given something as brilliant as a credit card. He found a crumpled bill.

"The phrase on the back. Read it aloud."

"In God we trust."

"You see!" God beamed triumphantly. "Trust is more valuable than money. In some ways it is more valuable than love. It is the currency of the soul."

David let the words sink in. He had never trusted anybody completely, not even his wife, whom he'd loved dearly. A friend once told him that the reason he'd gotten into the insurance business was because everyone always needed back-up. Trust was like back-up to Love.

"Gin!" cried the old woman behind David, startling him.

And God was gone. Out the window were only darkness and silver turbines. Or was She? From his seat pocket he heard a familiar voice:

"What say we play a hand as well?" God whispered. "And you can tell me all about the presentation in Los Angeles."

David reached into the seat pocket in front of him. As the flight was a long one they'd been given an assortment of items for amusement, including a deck of cards. David opened the pack.

The Queen of Hearts slid up and out on her own accord, winking at David. "Do you know how to play Solitaire?" God asked, straightening Her crown.

David nodded. He placed the Queen on a corner of his tray table and began setting other cards in the appropriate rows beside her.

"Excellent!" God retorted.

"It's you who is the card, my Lord." He began telling her of his fascinating day at Chloe Night. She seemed to want particulars so he started by describing the agency's idiosyncratic building. Funny, David thought. God could ride on the wing of a jetliner and occupy the persona of a playing card. Yet here she was asking questions about the presentation. Why hadn't she just attended?

God read his mind. "I hate meetings," she said. "Besides, this will allow us time to catch up."

It never ceased to amaze David the way God embraced the mundane. "Catching up? That seems so trivial in your grand scheme," David quipped, laying the Jack of Clubs beneath Her.

"Conversation is a passion of mine, David." God replied earnestly. "I've always wished it would shape this world more. For example, the discussion a man has with his psychiatrist. Meaningful dialogue. That is how I envisioned society. That is why I delight in our talks."

Maybe God's passion for language also explained Her penchant for using the King's English as opposed to say an American dialect.

"Funny, the advertising idea I saw earlier revolved around conversation. Things people say. Small talk that really wasn't small at all." He brought up the "How are you?" campaign. After all, it was such a common interrogative, perhaps beginning more conversations than any other.

A good segue, God listened raptly. She was most intrigued.

Unbeknownst to either, Evelyn listened as well, observing them through the slit of one unblinking, cat-like eye.

The plane banked up and to the left, avoiding the Rocky Mountains looming ahead.

TWENTY-THREE

THE third hole at Riviera Country Club was one of the easier ones, a long par four with little threat from the hazard. Two benign sand traps lay comfortably apart and away from the green.

Barry and Vernon approached the tee on foot. They'd forsaken carts this time out, both preferring to get some actual exercise. The goodwill from yesterday's meeting had given the men a boost. Each looked forward to carrying his clubs and breaking a sweat.

Vernon would have preferred using the agency membership at the Los Angeles Country Club but there were just too many unspoken policies there, whispers of racism. Barry nixed it, and Vernon obliged. And since there was no way he'd ever drive into the Valley, here they were: A couple miles from the agency, a well-heeled and debatably diverse membership, a few movie stars, Riviera made sense. Besides, with its perfectly coifed grounds and typically sparse population of golfers, Riviera hardly seemed like a compromise at all.

"All in all," Barry said, lining up his shot, "our presentation was flawless. A lot like this shot I'm about to make."

He hit the ball hard, nailing the sweet spot; it sailed a good 200 yards, maybe longer, and straight.

"Nice hit, Barry. As advertised."

Vernon put his ball on the tee. "Now what about a wretch like me?"

He slapped the ball. It sailed right but then careened off a tree, landing on the fairway just shy of Barry's.

"A miracle shot...you bastard!"

"Indeed." Vernon cheered. "God must be smiling on me." In addition to this fortuitous ricochet, he'd made par on the last hole as well, a first for him there. He slung his bag over his shoulder and headed up the fairway.

Barry followed, shaking his head in disbelief. Not so much at the lucky bounce his partner's ball had just taken, but in Vernon's bounce period. Nice to see the man happy for a change. It had been awhile since the two men played golf, or done anything together. All was right in the world. Yet, his partner was in more than a good mood; he seemed *transformed*. Barry quietly wondered if Vernon had somehow been cleansed when he got pushed in the pool, baptized!

And what about how good *he* was feeling? This morning he'd made love to his wife for the first time in months. What was going on there? How could yesterday's meeting be providing this much positive energy? They'd had lots of good meetings. The agency was known for them. Barry could only shake his head and marvel. Maybe Vernon was right. God was smiling on them both.

He caught up to Vernon and they walked along quietly, admiring the familiar but always comforting scenery, a cerulean sky you only found close to the ocean.

"That was a good thing you did earlier," Barry said.

Vernon stopped. "I've been taking lessons."

Barry laughed. "I meant hiring Luis."

They resumed walking. "It's a risk, I know," Vernon said. "But he's a good kid. Very bright. It was the right thing to do."

"No offense, Vern, but doing the right thing hasn't always been your credo."

"No offense taken. You seem chipper as well, Bar. Healthier."

"Funny that. I worked late on the pitch but I woke up feeling better than I have in years. Like someone rid my body of a terrible disease. I know this sounds queer but it feels good to be alive."

Two mourning doves swooped down from the trees, cooing as they flew, alighting on a shed. Vernon pointed to the birds. "You know, Bar, I used to think those doves were a nuisance…waking me up so damn early."

"I know what you mean," Barry said. "They're always congregating outside our bedroom window."

The pair of doves began cooing. "Hit the ball!' Hit the ball!" they seemed to be saying.

"Yes, well," Vernon added, "I know this is going to sound weird as well, but right now I think they're just about the most beautiful creatures I've ever seen."

"Wow, Vern. That's intense."

Barry had to laugh. Vernon Night did not say things like that. Not about birds, not about people, not about anything. But Barry became quiet when he remembered the story he'd made up for his daughter. The one in which she'd conjured up the Blue Bird of Happiness.

Vernon smiled beatifically. Barry's laughter hadn't bothered him at all. On the contrary, who wouldn't laugh? It's not like Vernon forgot what kind of a man he was.

"Tell me something Barry. Do you think there are any golf courses in Heaven?" Behind his back, he wrapped his arms around a seven iron, giving them a good stretch.

"I hadn't really thought about it," Barry replied. "I can't imagine you would have either." He'd never asked but he was certain Vernon was an atheist, agnostic at best.

"What about mourning doves, Barry? Such pretty creatures. I'd expect there'd be scores of them in Heaven."

Once again, his partner's treacle took him by surprise. As did their conversation in general. "What's going on here, Vern? You seem unduly joyous."

A foursome was setting up behind them and they had to continue moving.

Vernon slapped Barry on the shoulder. "Joyous, eh? Twenty bucks says I whip your ass today!"

Now that was more like the Vernon Night Barry knew. Barry sparked to the challenge.

"Why not make it twenty a hole, just for sport?"

"See your green at the green," Vernon said, approaching his ball.

Thinking God might very well be by his side, Vernon chose a wood. He was going for the pin.

"Mr. Night!"

Vernon's name sounded from behind him. He almost thought someone was warning him to duck. But then why not have yelled "Fore!"? And then closer: "Vernon Night?"

In disbelief, Vernon dropped his club. Barry put his iron back in the bag. For only the third time in as many years, he saw their other partner, Alex Wiener, heading toward them in a golf cart. In addition to driving too fast, the goon who drove the cart had on shades and a hoodie…and zero regard for course protocol.

But, then, neither did Alex.

"May I have a word with you, Vernon?" the old man said, dispensing with any niceties. "It won't take long."

"Of course, Mr. Wiener," Vernon replied, nervously picking up his club. Like there was any way he'd say no.

"It's pronounced winner," the goon corrected him.

Vernon extended the senior partner his hand. "How are you, sir?"

It went unshaken. "Never mind all that. I need to talk to you."

Vernon didn't ask about the man who was driving the cart and no introductions were given. He spoke, trying to remain calm, "You remember, Barry Fine."

"Hello." Barry said, keeping his hands by his side.

Wiener ignored Barry. "I need you to get in the cart, Vernon." He adjusted his sunglasses. They were thick, big and dark, the kind you saw worn by the villain in an old James Bond movie. "Without your assistant."

"Barry's not my assistant. He's-"

"In the cart, please." Wiener showed no emotion.

The goon was a statue.

Vernon looked helplessly at Barry before getting in the cart.

"I'll be right back, Bar."

The goon fired up the cart and they sped down the fairway.

"As you may know, I've never been much of a fan of our Hebrew associate." Wiener coughed into his gloved hand. "I prefer your *countenance*."

Hebrew? Countenance?

"Excuse me sir, but in addition to being my partner, Barry is also the Chief Creative Officer at CN&W."

"Ah yes. The entertainment portion of our little venture."

So much for Vernon's "unduly joyous" mood.

"In case you didn't know, sir, our reputation is built on creative. Your millions come from it." Vernon spoke his mind but he had to be careful. In addition to being a partner, Alex Wiener was also the number one shareholder.

They stopped in front of Vernon's ball.

Wiener didn't flinch. He brushed aside Vernon's defense of Barry. "I suppose every organ grinder must have his monkey."

In lieu of teeing off on the old man with his driver, Vernon methodically removed the club from its bag, got out of the cart, sized up his shot, took it, watched it fall just short of the green, and returned.

"Okay, then," he said evenly. "To what do *I* owe the pleasure of your visit?"

"The meeting with Happy Soul. It went well?"

A big picture guy, the old man seldom paid attention to any one account at CN&W and that included pitches. So what was this about? "It went real, real well," Vernon answered, his straightforward tone belying true curiosity.

"Unfortunately, we won't be moving forward with them."

"We won't?"

"The Happy Soul Industry is not a viable client. Get back in the cart, Vernon."

"I thought you said this wouldn't take long," Vernon said curtly, beginning to lose his patience. Nevertheless, he got back in the cart.

"I'm afraid HSI is in direct conflict with other agency interests."

Vernon rolled his eyes. "What could be more interesting to the agency than new business?"

"There's a conflict."

"Another client?" Vernon asked. "Not possible. We did the diligence."

The cart stopped in front of the golf ball. Weiner continued:

"I'm afraid it's a shareholder matter. It's also a done deal. Is that understood?" It wasn't phrased as a question.

Vernon was speechless. He could have asked more questions. He could have asked why. Instead he just sat there, dumbstruck. He knew Wiener wasn't going to explain himself further. His edicts came down even more infrequently than he did. And they were always obeyed. Both he and Barry thought it was a pretty small price to pay for the relative autonomy they regularly enjoyed.

Solemnly, Vernon got out of the cart.

"Chip on with a choked-up nine," the goon said.

Instead of playing the ball, Vernon headed back toward his partner.

They both met in the middle of the fairway.

"What happened?" Barry asked.

"We're off Happy Soul. No explanation."

Like an irate golfer, Barry thumped his club on the ground, kicking up sod.

"I don't know what to say," Vernon said.

"How about Wiener's a dick?" Barry said, pretty much nailing it.

"And we were having such a perfect day," observed Vernon. "A perfect week."

Barry watched another pair of mourning doves bickering on the fairway. Even they had turned foul. "God giveth and God taketh away, eh Vern?"

"We're still blessed, amigo," Vernon said. "If we can't work on Happy Soul we've got a lot of other clients. I can't help but think they'll benefit from our work on the pitch. We all will."

"Wiener's still a dick, though." Barry said.

"Yes he is, Barry. Yes he is."

TWENTY-FOUR

BECAUSE of favorable tailwinds (and perhaps an assist from the Lord), David and Evelyn's flight had arrived nearly two hours early, at just before three o'clock in the morning, Eastern time. So early, in fact, that a gate wasn't available at JFK and they had to land at LaGuardia instead.

As soon as they exited the aircraft, Evelyn got on her mobile, informing the car service of their premature arrival and destination change. "No problem," she told David. "They've got a car available right now."

"Marvelous," David said, but he wasn't really listening. He found himself too distracted by the lowly surroundings. Toward the end of his actual life, traveling by air had become a romantic dream come true. And while he recognized that the skies were now available to everyone instead of an affluent few, he still thought that this airport to America's most famous city could do better than LaGuardia.

At this ungodly hour, under its sickly, bluish lights, the frazzled and straggling passengers looked more like zombies stumbling around in a morgue. Litter was strewn about the gate corridor and some of the walls had been defaced by graffiti. Large, shiny ads hawking antacid and electronic gadgets gleamed inappropriately from lighted display cases, their promises of calmer stomachs and "connectivity" appearing dubious in such a grubby environment. More passed out than sleeping, a man lay forlornly atop a chair in the corner. Doubtful he was waiting for plane or passenger. The sign at baggage claim said "Welcome to New York!" The ambiance said, "Get the hell out!"

"No offense, Ms. Warren. But your airport is a disappointment."

"Think of it as the mud room to a fabulous palace."

David chuckled. "Good answer."

At baggage claim, he watched the bags come thumping out from behind tired rubber flaps, almost like the airport itself were defecating luggage.

The baggage security officer was at her post, but dozing. Nobody seemed to care. Folks just got their bags and got out. If David had been aware of homeland security, he would have wondered about the breakdown here. Granted, the hour was very early and they were an atypical arrival, but still...

As it was, they took advantage of lax security and were out in a flash.

The long, white limousine awaited them, alone at the curb. Evelyn's last name, spelled incorrectly, was pasted on the window.

"Damn," Evelyn retorted. "I specifically told them no stretches."

But David smiled. "It certainly is big." He was excited. He'd never been in a limousine like this before and he could not hide his boyish enthusiasm.

"Thank God nobody's awake too see us." Evelyn handed the driver her bag. She didn't wait for him to open the door.

"Good evening, my good man!" David chimed to the driver, wanting a little more drama from his limousine experience.

"It's morning," the driver said with a grudge. He tossed David's suitcase in the trunk on top of an oilcan. He seemed more accustomed to Evelyn's approach.

"Well then, top of the morning to you!" David refused to come down from his natural high. He was an angel and did not require sleep, so he was wide-awake and raring to go. And while he understood the driver's apathy, he waited patiently for him to come around and open his door. Surely, some remnant of luxury existed?

Evelyn was on the phone again. David couldn't imagine to whom she was talking at this time of the morning but he refrained from asking.

She hung up quickly. "Just checking my voicemail," she said. "I've got clients overseas. It's the middle of the day for some."

David nodded. Evelyn was a busy woman. He understood she had other clients and he wasn't going to hold checking up on them against her. Still, he couldn't help but notice how she had an edge about her now, a quickness. It was palpable.

Unfortunately, the limo, like the airport, did not live up to David's expectations. The car's interior was an off-putting combination of spill-stained lacquer and worn imitation leather.

"77th east of Madison," Evelyn told the driver. "Take the bridge." She leaned back not anticipating a reply. "One good thing about arriving at this hour: No traffic."

As they headed away from the airport, David could only imagine the sea of cars that would envelop this road in a matter of hours. Out the window he saw his first glimpse, in years, of the imposing skyline of Manhattan. He recognized the Empire State Building, where they'd soon be going. He was surprised to see so many other structures nearly as tall, some even taller.

Then something peculiar: two identical, mammoth towers loomed left in the skyline. Not real anymore, just their aura. Something terrible had happened there. Out of fear of being seen as naïve, he refrained from asking about them.

He settled into his seat, saying nothing. Los Angeles had struck him as a silly place, superficial and shiny. But New York was more than just geographically opposite. It was tonally the antithesis as well.

Dark, fierce and intimidating, New York would take getting used to, all over again.

Even so, when they crossed the Triborough Bridge, beginning their swing into the city, he felt his spirit soar. More than a palace, it was as if he were entering a kingdom.

And apparently it was a kingdom with "roadwork ahead."

Almost surrealistically, they came to a standstill.

The driver didn't wait to be questioned about it. "Night shift," he said. "Could be tough all the way."

"Damn," Evelyn muttered, under her breath. If the driver knew about the construction then why the hell hadn't he suggested an alternative? She figured it was useless questioning the chauffeur, let alone berating him.

"You want I take bridge, I take bridge," he said, providing an alibi for his behavior. Without even being questioned, he'd gotten defensive.

They inched along as if in a funeral procession.

"The city that never sleeps…" David sighed. The words just came naturally – even though David was unaware of Frank Sinatra.

"Let's get off here," Evelyn cut in. Exasperated, she did not have a problem commanding the driver. "We'll cut through Harlem."

The angel's eyes opened wide. He remembered Harlem from its rambunctious, jazz-filled swing clubs and speakeasies. His wife had been fond of jazz music, and even though their friends disapproved, she'd played the phonograph constantly.

The driver knew another Harlem, a far meaner one. He turned around and stared at Evelyn, saying nothing.

She did the same to him. Many seconds ticked…

"You want this way?" He pulled out of line, taking the 110th Street exit. "I take this way."

They weren't the only people making that particular move but they were definitely in the minority. Upon entering the surface streets of Harlem, their minority status increased even more.

Overall scantily populated, pockets of people congregated in groups on the corners, in alcoves and doorways. What they were doing was not apparent. Most of them did, however, take immediate notice of the white limousine as it paraded through their shattered stretch of real estate. They followed the car with unblinking eyes, the way a cat does when it first observes a mouse.

Click. The driver power-locked the doors.

"I always thought Harlem would be more festive." David said, not knowing what to make of this place and these people. He was reminded of the airport's sordid conditions, and now these people, out on the street and every single one of them black.

"It's a good shortcut. Surely, you've taken it before?" Evelyn sounded incredulous. Her lover and potential client seemed to be in wonder of everything.

Ahead of them a green light went yellow and their driver sped up. At the last second, he hit the brakes hard. They didn't make it.

The car sat by itself at the intersection. The sky was showing its first bit of daylight, a pale blue. Shame no one in the car noticed.

On the corner three young men stared at them. One pointed.

And then a knock on David's window.

David's limo in L.A. had a nifty switch that automatically opened its windows and he found one similar to it here. "Hello," he said, to the outlandishly attired, heavily made-up, dark-skinned woman. "Are you in need of something?"

"Are you crazy man?" the driver blurted. "Shut the Goddamn window!"

The hooker didn't hear him. She answered David by reiterating his question verbatim. "Are *you* in need of anything?"

Ignoring the driver, she sized up the two passengers, and smiled at what she saw. She'd done more than a few uptown couples looking for a thrill. They were easy money, safe and quick. Most times only one of the two got busy. The other would watch. White folks liked to watch.

"You all looking for some chocolate aren't you? A little late night snack?" She lifted her leg up to the window, rolling down her fishnet stockings, showing off her ample thigh.

David loved chocolate. But he got an idea that the sweets being offered here were far from confectionery.

The prostitute wasted no time with her opportunity – other hookers, thugs, even the police were around every corner. Having done so a thousand times, she reached down into the open window and found the door handle. Quickly, she lifted it, freeing the lock. The door opened and she was in.

"Hey lover," the woman said, running her hands over David. She was looking for money with one hand and his penis with the other. She continued to ignore the limo driver who was yelling at her: "Get out! Get out! Get out!"

"How you doin', honey?" she asked Evelyn over David's shoulder, sizing her up while groping him. "Hmmm, you two look like you know how to have a good time."

"Please ma'am!" David pleaded. He pushed her away but she was inexorable. "You're making a mistake. We're not looking for a good time-"

"That's right baby 'cause you already found it." She pulled his shirt bottom out of his pants. At this point, regardless of what transpired next, she knew she was going to get paid. Even if it was just to get out of the car.

The driver was hysterical. From behind the protective glass, he held his head between his hands, moaning, as he watched in horror the goings-on in the back. Obviously, he wanted the prostitute gone but what could he do? There was no way he was going to exit the car's relative safety and try to drag her away. He was a fairly small man and weaponless as well. And this was fucking Harlem! On top of that, because of immigration issues, he was afraid to even radio the police. The driver had no choice but to do what he was paid to do. He put the car in gear.

"If it's money you want we'll give you money," David said, sliding out from under the hooker and onto the floor. He backed toward the opposite seats clambering onto them. He was breathing heavily, and almost in shock. If he had any angelic powers, they were lost to him now. Forgotten anyway. "Evelyn," he gasped. "Do you have something you can give her...*please*?"

Both he and the prostitute looked expectantly at her purse.

Evelyn, who'd been silent throughout the whole ordeal, finally spoke. "Yes, David, I have something for our friend but I'm afraid she's going to have to earn it."

She faced the hooker, grinning lasciviously. Slowly, Evelyn undid the top button of her blouse, and then the second button...

"Tsk-tsk," clucked the prostitute. "I had you two figured all wrong. I got me a naughty girl, don't I?" She said it again, louder, this time moving toward her. "Don't I, baby?"

"Hmm, hmm," Evelyn purred.

"This is going to cost you, sugar," the hooker said, moving into her arms.

The limousine driver slowed down, craning his neck to partake of this latest turn of events. He all but stopped when he saw the two women come together and kiss.

It happened fast. Grasping the whore hard around her torso, Evelyn swung the woman to the other side of her seat. The car door opened, and with one powerful shove, the hooker was jettisoned onto the street.

"Drive," she said to the driver. "Before she gets up."

Flummoxed, the chauffeur did not have to be told twice.

David looked up. "I can't believe you just did that," he said to Evelyn, his eyes still on the wobbly prostitute.

"What, kiss her?" Evelyn replied, sarcastically. "Neither can I."

"Good thing the car was moving so slowly or she'd be-"

"In a better place," Evelyn said.

David sat down beside Evelyn, collapsing really. He half-heartedly tried to tuck his shirt back in. He saw his belt on the floor but lacked the energy to get it. For someone who did not require sleep he was utterly spent.

"Did she get your wallet?" Evelyn asked, fixing her face and hair.

The angel didn't carry one (only the lone credit card and a driver's license) but he just said "No."

Mercifully the car left Harlem into the stunningly contrary environs of Central Park. Even in bare light, one could easily tell how lush and well kept the park was. Lichen-encrusted stone edifices butted out over the road, topped with shrubbery and trees. If not for the occasional, glorious spires of certain buildings showing through the foliage, it would appear they were in the European countryside, which was, of course, what the park's creator, Frederick Law Olmsted, had intended.

"What a world." David said. "What a world."

TWENTY-FIVE

NOT trusting the neighborhood, Erin Night parked her new Lexus as close as she could to the front entrance. After all, she wasn't too far from where her estranged husband had been carjacked.

She was in West Hollywood, sort of, east of La Cienega and south of Wilshire Boulevard. It was the kind of neighborhood you never thought of until for some reason you found yourself in it. Neither overtly bad nor good, it seemed more like an unhappy middle. There were no liquor stores or pawnshops. Nobody was hanging around. Yet there wasn't anything pleasant about the place either. The yards all seemed dead, or dying, with no sign of children or dogs.

Erin reached inside her purse in order to verify the address as well as confirm the presence of her mace spray.

Reassured, she got out of the car and hurriedly made her way to the Mandalay Courts apartment complex.

The modernistic, pseudo-tropical building was exactly where she would have expected to find a guy like Phil, only in her mind it might not have been so dilapidated. The complex reminded her of a shoddy version of "Melrose Place." The pool had been drained ages ago, and, in lieu of a comely cast, only refuse lay around it. Three of the four palm trees on the parkway had expired into barren poles, the remaining one well on its way.

The dreary atmosphere only made her feel worse about what she had done at the CN&W office party. Convincing that drunken kid to push Vern in the pool had cost him his job. Which pretty much ensured that he'd be unable to leave the Mandalay Courts anytime soon.

At first, she was surprised by her nagging guilt over the subject, assuming a decade-long bad marriage had pureed what was left of her conscience. But her feelings of shame had only increased with each passing day, even hour.

After Vernon split, Erin's obsession with Phillip grew unbearable, eventually driving her to his home, where she found herself now.

Erin discovered his name on the buzzer panel: Phillip Connors. It had been written by hand, inordinately florid, especially given the surroundings. She took a deep breath, wondering if she should take another Valium.

Erin pushed the button and waited.

And waited.

She pushed it again and just when she was about to turn around and leave, the door opened.

"Sorry, the intercom doesn't really work anymore," Phillip said. "Like a lot of things around here."

Even though it was mid-afternoon, it looked like the man had been sleeping. Phil was unkempt, unshaved, wearing a pair of crumpled khaki shorts and a Joe Camel tee shirt. Flip-flops.

When he noticed the striking blonde at his door (as opposed to the Fed Ex guy) he stood up straight, doing what he could to improve his appearance. He tried to tuck in his shirt, but without a belt it only worsened things. Feeling awkward, he put his hands in his pockets.

"What can I do for you?"

"You don't recognize me, do you?"

"Um…" Phil scanned his memory – in turns provoked by what he might find there as well as worried. An attractive, older woman was not on his radar so what was she doing on his doorstep?

"I'm sorry."

"It's understandable," Erin said. "You were pretty well smashed at the time. Not to mention employed." She hurt for a cigarette and had to believe Phillip did so as well. These were cigarette-smoking moments.

Phil experienced a clearing in his head. "The party. How did you know about that?"

And then it hit him.

Needless to say, Phil stopped feeling insecure about the woman on his doorstep. He shook his head up and down, nodding vigorously. Tapped the air in front of her face with his index finger. "You're *her!* You're Vernon Night's wife!"

"Ex-wife." Erin said, pulling out the cigarette and lighting it. "We're separated."

Phillip stopped shaking. Bit his lower lip. "Like I said before: What the hell can I do for you?"

She ignored the attitude. He was entitled. She deserved his wrath. And anyway, living with Vernon, she'd heard it all before.

"Actually, it's more what I can do for you."

"Where have I heard that before?" Phillip smirked. "Oh, yeah, from you."

"May I come in?"

"Then what?" Phil asked. He was jaded enough to actually angle for sex. The numbing array of pornography he'd ingested lately hadn't helped his reasoning abilities either.

"You can find out," she said, "by asking me in." A gray plume of smoke drifted up from her cigarette in the tepid afternoon air.

"Seems to me..." Phillip said, "that the last time I did what you asked, my life took a serious turn for the worse."

"I'm acutely aware of that, Phillip. And I'm sorry. And that's why I'm here."

"Coming through!" A corpulent older man in a green velour sweat-suit excused himself around the two and went bouncing down the sidewalk. He smelled improbably of fried bacon and cigars.

"Come on in," Phil sighed. "It's not like I have anything else to lose." Part of him was still holding out for the massage.

She followed him up the stairs, struck by the aroma of mildew. It dominated the corridor, even over the previous man's cigar.

"Forgive the place," Phil said before they even entered. "I had to let the interior decorator go."

Once again, she allowed the asides. Funny, she thought, how hard that had been with Vernon. She'd stepped on so many of his jokes and witticisms eventually they'd turned into snide cracks, grousing. Erin shuddered. What if, at least partially, she'd created the vile person her husband had become?

Phil cleared the debris from his forlorn couch. "It's shabby sans chic. Have a seat. There's an ashtray underneath the couch."

He went to the window and released the blind, allowing some sun to come in. "Can I get you a drink? I've got orange juice, club soda, Bud Light, Mountain Dew-"

"Champagne?"

"It's not chilled," Phil deadpanned.

"Sorry, Phillip," Erin said, meaning it. *Champagne? What was she thinking?*

"Living in LA can make you stupid. Very stupid."

"That's okay," Phillip smiled. He appreciated she had used his proper name and that she was making fun of herself.

"Hey, you know what? I've got some sparkling wine. It's good. From my dad's vineyards."

"Wonderful." Erin knew that Phillip's father was the CEO of Meritage Wines. She'd even met him once. He owned the third larg-est vineyard in Northern California and was CN&W's oldest client.

Thanks to Jack Connors, Phillip had obtained his gig at the agency. She wondered if Phil had told his father about his change in job status and all the embarrassing circumstances surrounding it. She doubted it. Jack was strictly old school and would probably have disowned him. She bet even Vernon hadn't called the old man yet.

Phillip came back to the living room carrying a bottle and two glasses. "It's five o'clock somewhere, right?"

He flopped down beside his guest and prepared their drinks. He handed her a flute, one of the dozen his mother had gifted him. "So, what brings you to the Mandalay? If it's to say you're sorry, you're too late... I'm sorrier."

"I am sorry, Phillip. It was a terrible thing for me to do."

"Vernon didn't like it much either."

"No."

They sat silently for a moment.

Phil brought his glass to hers. "Well then," he said. "To new beginnings!"

"Hear, hear!" Erin responded, taking a generous swig.

"You want to know the truth about it, Mrs. Night?"

"Call me Erin. And yes."

"The truth is, Erin, I never liked that job. I know it's an old song but I only took the position to appease my father." He lifted his glass up into the sunlight, spotless from lack of use, though dusty. "It was either that or pick his damn grapes."

Erin knew Phillip was not being facetious. Jack Connors would love nothing more than to see his son in the field. She was more surprised by his comment regarding the job. It seemed everybody wanted a job in advertising and, in particular, at CN&W.

"Didn't you like the agency?" she asked.

"Chloe Night was great," Phillip replied. "I just didn't like the business."

"You mean all the politics?"

Erin had heard her share of interdepartmental horror stories from Vernon. She'd deduced that in a business where nothing was manufactured, people justified their existence in other ways, many ridiculous, and all of them political. Sometimes she'd gotten the impression – even from Vernon – that it was easier and more lucrative to have meetings about advertising as opposed to actually making any.

"There's politics everywhere, Erin. I'm talking about the concept of advertising itself."

He pulled a cigarette out from his own pack. Lit it.

"I'm no communist but marketing at that level freaks me out. You have all these specialists looking for targets, assessing them for vulnerabilities, and then turning around and creating exactly the right weapon…it's creepy."

Erin laughed. "Well, when you put it *that way*."

"That is the way. That's advertising." Smoke blew out of his nostrils like a snort from a bull.

"What is it you would like to do then, if it's not advertising or wine making?" Erin washed over the room with her eyes. Surely, lounging around here wasn't his end-all.

Phillip poured both of them more wine. "I don't know. I like to play guitar. Jazz guitar."

He pointed to a row of instruments leaning up against the wall. "I would be happy just mastering the craft. Maybe teaching. Playing in a band on weekends."

Phillip tapped his cigarette ash into the tray until every piece of gray was gone. Only the ember remained. "I need more lessons. But the old man thinks that it's a waste of time… no money in jazz."

Music had once been important to Erin as well. Of all things, she played the harp; the gilded instrument was still tipped up against the wall in her basement. Erin made a mental note to retrieve it.

"Maybe I can help."

Phillip got up and went over to his motley collection. He selected a ratty vintage Fender. "It's not a jazz guitar but if this thing were in better shape it would be worth a fortune." He pulled out a pick from its neck and began strumming.

"I can't hear it." Erin didn't care that he hadn't acknowledged her offer. She would prefer he played his guitar.

"Owner won't let me plug in on Sundays. Says it's disrespectful.

He's kind of a religious freak." Phillip stopped talking, leaned over his instrument and soloed for a while.

Though she barely made out the notes, clearly Phillip was hearing something. Erin wondered if it was a known standard or some obtuse jazz piece from the avant-garde period. She sat back and let him play. Would pushing Vernon into a pool someday lead Phillip onto a stage? Fate could be funny that way. Right when you're in a groove (good or bad) something unexpected always happened – not unlike the meandering flow of a piece of jazz music.

"What was my husband paying you?" Erin asked, when he was done.

"Well, actually, I didn't work for your husband."

Erin rolled her eyes. "Then how much was the guy you worked for paying you?"

"It wasn't a guy," Phil rebuked, playfully aware. The glass of wine had gone to his head, as had his playing.

"Seriously," she said.

"The answer is not very much. If I was into it more I probably could have gotten more. But I wasn't and I didn't." He walked the guitar back to its stand and lovingly put it on the stand.

"I got a friend at the Blue Note," Phillip said, returning to and settling back in his seat. "He's offered me work behind the bar. Maybe he'll even let me play. The pay, as you might imagine, sucks. But, like I said, he might even let me play." Phillip laughed. "I'd rather serve wine than make it."

Erin smiled. She hadn't been sure of what she was going to do before she'd arrived. But now she was certain. Reaching into her purse, she got out her checkbook and started writing.

"I'll need to call my broker but this should clear in a week. It's for $25,000." She dropped the check in his lap.

"You know you don't have to do this. I mean I pushed him, not you."

"And it was worth every penny. I want you to take those lessons. Buy yourself a real guitar."

She stood up. "Phillip, I'm sorry for what I did. And I'm tired of feeling sorry."

"A new start?" Phillip mused, too stunned to get up.

"No more advertising for either of us," Erin added. "Maybe we both get what we want in the end. Call it fate."

They toasted glasses – her standing, him sitting.

"You know what they say, Erin. There are no coincidences."

"Who said that?"

"I'm not sure," Phillip replied. "It may be from a song."

"No money in those," Erin laughed.

"I'm not so sure," Phillip countered, running his fingers over Erin's check.

TWENTY-SIX

THE biggest difference between East Coast agencies and West Coast agencies was that in New York they didn't even bother trying to be cool, a little because they were the big boys but mostly because they could never pull it off anyway. Selling out wasn't even a valid phrase on Madison Avenue. Selling product was. And the better they did that, the better they did. Even though the Empire State Building was off Madison Avenue, Town & Robertson was still that kind of a place.

Evelyn and David were led into a grand conference room, beautifully appointed. Frank Lloyd Wright–inspired cherry wood cabinetry wrapped around all four walls. A massive array of electronic and computer hardware was centered on the far wall of the room. In addition, flat-screen, steel-cased monitors hung from every corner. The space had obviously been rigged for teleconferencing; a conspicuous camera hung from the center portion of the ceiling on a swivel. This was clearly the boardroom Town & Robertson used for only the most particular of occasions, new business presentations being one of them.

A sumptuous buffet stretched atop a jet-black console. Smoked salmon rippled pink on an ornate silver tray. A flow of black caviar followed, augmented by bagels, toast, and other accoutrements.

"The advantages of going public," Evelyn said, cognizant of how ostentatious it all looked. David liked fine things (her automobile and the Four Seasons among them) but he was not a pompous man. She worried that the Platinum Room was coming across as a bit much.

"Are you hungry?" she asked, motioning to the spread as if she even had to.

David hadn't an appetite. But then, even amongst the living, the act of eating often had little to do with appetites. And now was a good example. He knew the lavish spread was merely part of meeting protocol, something somebody was told to bring in. It had been set up and paid for, part of an arrangement or contract. Tampax and Unilever got the same treatment. That was the cost of doing business.

Still, David loathed that the food should go uneaten. He remembered his mother's admonition that "children were starving in China," an ancient cliché but he also knew it was true. As an ambassador of goodwill he hated waste of any kind.

When alive, he'd brunched with a Jewish fellow from the office more than a few times. From these outings, David recognized the bagels, cream cheese, and lox and made himself a sandwich.

"Good for you!" Evelyn said. "Usually people look at the salmon like it's still swimming."

"There's enough fish here to feed a multitude."

David thought about how Jesus had doled out one fish to so many, and grimaced. It was one of God's earliest myths and, in his mind, one of her best. She'd hate (hate being a relative word) that an entire salmon had been utilized as mere fodder for a business meeting.

"Where would you like me to sit?" David asked, self-consciously. There were at least twenty chairs wrapping around the room's massive table.

"Anywhere is fine," she said to him, pointing to the nearest seat. "We can do our presentation from either side."

"Won't you join me?" he said, pensively. They'd shared a great deal over the last few days. He hoped it hadn't become all business.

Evelyn said nothing. Like him, Evelyn wasn't hungry but she could eat if she had to. She considered the earthbound angel. His black hair appeared to be showing a hint of gray and she wondered how that was possible. Had she begun to age as well?

"Of course," she replied, taking a number of melon slices off the buffet and organizing them on the company's fine monogrammed china. Beneath the T&R logo were the words "Excellence through Persuasion." She placed a blueberry muffin on top of them.

The two sat and ate in silence, mulling the events about to take place. One thought he knew what was going to happen and the other was certain of it.

And yet, neither would be prepared.

David had been fairly blown away by Chloe Night's presentation and had told God as much. Yet, he fully expected an equally impressive display from T&R. Present company in mind, he was hoping for one as well. He dabbed the sides of his mouth with a linen napkin before speaking.

"Tell me again, Evelyn, about the people I'm going to meet."

That they were even here had been an act of spontaneity. David had accrued only a modicum of information about the agency or its leadership. He knew from his talks with God that it was among the very largest advertising agencies in the world, with offices around the globe, numerous partners and subsidiaries, and billings in the billions. But he did not know anything really about its management. Just that there were a lot of them, all made quite wealthy by the recent public offering. He'd never broached the subject with Evelyn but he had every reason to believe that she was a millionaire as well. The thought made him uneasy but he shook it off. It was not fair to link success with badness. God helped those who helped themselves.

It was as if Evelyn could read his mind.

"It's a very big company, David," she said. "There are a lot of players." Evelyn folded her napkin and placed it on top of her plate. "My inclination is that you will be received by our top man." She checked her watch. "And soon."

"The Chief Executive is going to present creative? Isn't that a bit unorthodox?"

Though Barry and Vernon had pitched him in LA, David felt that that was somehow different. They *were* the show at CN&W; one of them even had his name on the door. There was no Mr. Town or Mr. Robertson. Leastwise living.

"You're special, David," Evelyn answered, smiling. "The CEO wants to meet you himself. When he found out you were coming to see us he cleared his calendar. He made a special trip up." She poured herself a glass of ice water, the splashing and tinkling pronounced against the crystal.

"Up?" David asked.

Evelyn's smile flickered. "Nathan was in Florida. He has a place there. He likes the warm climate."

"I'm flattered."

Nathan Moor was indeed the agency's Chief Executive Officer as well as the subject of the one article David had read about T&R. Mr. Moor was widely credited with resuscitating the agency from its doldrums in the early Nineties, consummated, of course, by a very lucrative IPO just last year. He was considered a maverick and a ruthless negotiator. He was not, however, a creative person.

"Will he be showing me the advertising or just chairing the meeting?" David wondered. He was asking a lot of questions but he supposed that's what clients did. In the short time he'd been immersed in this project he'd already noticed how profoundly different account people were from creative. According to the magazine article Nathan Moor was the King of the Suits.

"My understanding is that he'll be showing you everything," Evelyn responded. "Nathan is an excellent presenter by the way. He can be very persuasive." Evelyn considered what she'd said, then added: "He's been a salesman all his life."

David tightened the knot on his tie in anticipation of meeting this great man. "An old school kind of guy, eh?"

"The oldest," she replied.

The angel thought about God's conversations with David Ogilvy and Leo Burnett. These were vintage ad guys and even though God had recommended HSI go another way, David was glad to at least be having an opportunity to hear from someone similar.

Evelyn got up, taking her plate with her. She emptied its contents into a shiny silver garbage can and then set the dirty plate down on the farthest corner of the buffet.

"Nathan doesn't like mess," she said almost respectfully. She moved it this way and that, seemingly struggling to find the right spot. She checked her watch.

"Are you all right?" David came up beside her with his plate in hand. He placed it directly on top of the one she'd been fiddling with, stopping her. Then he put his hand on hers. Or tried to. "You seem tense all of a sudden."

"It's an important meeting," she said, pulling away. "And he's an important man." She toyed with the fingers on her left hand, cracking knuckles.

David put an arm around her shoulder. It was almost the only physical contact they'd shared all day. "Hey, Nathan is the one who should be nervous. After all, he's presenting to me." He laughed, trying to lighten the mood. "I'm the client!" But it seemed to have the opposite effect.

Evelyn took his hand and removed it from her person. "Nathan doesn't get nervous David...*Ever.*"

"Okaaaay," David drawled. The hand she'd grabbed was tingling strangely. He hadn't seen this side of Evelyn before. She seemed pensive, cat-like. Even her features had taken on an edge. What once was curvy now seemed angular. Her hair appeared to be tighter to her forehead.

David checked his watch. The last thing he wanted to do was start this off poorly but he couldn't help but feel a tad miffed. He returned to the table and sat down.

"Well, whether he's nervous or not, he's late." David folded his hands on the table. He was sulking but who could blame him? Evelyn was behaving oddly, and had been ever since they'd arrived. Was Nathan a boyfriend too? What did it all add up to?

"FORGIVE ME, MR. Angelo. I'm afraid tardiness is one of my many bad habits." And with that pronouncement, in walked the Chief Executive Officer and primary shareholder of Town & Robertson, Nathan Moor.

For a big man, Nathan moved quickly. Before David could get up Nathan was behind him, hands upon his shoulders. "I trust you will find it in your heart to forgive me. You are the forgiving kind, are you not?" He laughed robustly and proceeded to shake David so hard that he forgot all about his tingling hand.

"Yes…well…" David wasn't sure how to deal with this boisterous, flamboyant hulk of a man.

With longish red hair and piercing green eyes, Nathan was as handsome as he was big. In addition to being physically intimidating, he exuded confidence and charisma. How else could he have gotten away with such a greeting? What person (especially a chief executive) walks up to a complete stranger (especially a new business prospect) and puts his hands upon him?

In effect, they felt more like two paws bearing down on David's back. As improbable as it sounded, for a moment David thought he was going to be pushed into the table.

And then the hands were off of him.

David turned around slowly, looking up at his unusual host.

"Welcome to New York City, Mr. Angelo! Welcome to Town & Robertson!" He spoke loudly, in a theatrical way, as if saying lines. He grinned, revealing, ever so briefly, a misshapen and decrepit set of teeth, his only flaw.

Quickly, he turned to the buffet. "I see you've eaten. Marvelous! As an advertising executive I encourage appetites of all kinds."

Was this normal behavior for a modern New Yorker? Evermore confused, for the first time since becoming a mortal David felt a sense of ego. Who did this arrogant man think he was? I'm the client, thought David.

"Hello, Nathan," Evelyn said evenly. She'd been expecting as much from her boss. "This is David Angelo. He is the Vice-President of Marketing at Happy-"

"Yes, of course he is. And how are you, Eve?" Nathan sniffed, cutting her off.

Evelyn moved closer to him, as if being drawn.

"Sit down, Eve."

She sat, falling into the nearest chair. Bowing her head, she said nothing. It was like she'd been turned off.

Yet, Nathan asked the question again, this time emphasizing each word: "How...Are...You?" But he wasn't directing the interrogative toward Evelyn. He wasn't even looking at her anymore. "Such a universal question: How are you? So mundane. So utterly *human*. Everyone uses the phrase. But what if people actually meant it? That would make a grand positioning for Happy Soul Industry, don't you think?"

David stared at Evelyn.

She remained still, not looking up.

How did Nathan know about Chloe Night's creative? Clearly, he was mocking them. Had she violated his confidence? If so, when? The short form of her name, Eve, was equally provocative.

"So *Eve*," David said, using the abbreviation of her name for the first time. "I didn't realize the contents of my other meeting were relevant to these proceedings. They were certainly confidential." Angels, as a rule, didn't get pissed off but David was feeling something akin to it now.

Eve shut her eyes, ashamed. What happened to the forceful creature David had come to know so intimately?

"You tell Eve, you tell me." Nathan said, matter-of-factly.

"Is that true, Evelyn?" David's voice was breaking. Had this woman really betrayed him?

Silence. Conspicuous outside as well. No cars honked. No sirens brayed. Just quiet. They were high up the tall building but it seemed odd not being able to hear an inkling of the world's busiest city.

"I'm sure Eve would love to answer you, David...If only she were living and breathing as opposed to, well...*not.*"

Something was wrong. David moved quickly to his lover's side. He said her name. He shook her. But Evelyn remained unresponsive. "What in God's name is going on here?" David barked, directing the question to both of them.

Evelyn stirred, raising her head slowly to David. Her lips parted but no words came out. Instead, Eve's face began to draw into her mouth like water pouring into a drain. First her lips and chin and nose slipped into the widening orifice and then, like two stones in a rushing stream, her eyes. Soon she swallowed herself and was gone. Only the wardrobe remained in a rumpled pile on the chair, her scarf on the floor.

"Well now, Mr. Angelo. Would you like to know all about Eve?" Nathan asked, stepping toward him. He smiled, again revealing his vile teeth.

David could not answer. He was paralyzed, not so much from fear but by reckoning. He had witnessed a great many things in his life, and in the hereafter, but certainly nothing like this foul display.

"As it happens, Eve and I go way back," Nathan continued, his malevolent grin once again on display. He picked up Evelyn's clothes and folded them precisely. Then he took his own jacket off and placed it neatly on a chair back.

"It's hot in here, don't you think?" He smiled again. Like Sardonicus, he was always smiling. "Nothing wrong with a little heat, I always say, as long as you're prepared for it. Are you prepared for a little heat, Mr. Angelo?"

David did feel it getting warmer in the room. It was the first sense of temperature he'd experienced since returning to life. He felt something trickling down his side. Could he really be sweating? Scared, he ran his fingers across his brow. There too, wetness.

Nathan jumped on the boardroom table as effortlessly as a gazelle clearing a hedge. "Eve is one of my creations, Mr. Angelo. Or should I say *was*." He snorted, his lips rippling strangely. "She is what the earthborn call a succubus. Eve has seduced many men for me including, if the myths are correct, the first one of all."

Nathan licked his lips, his tongue wetly running around them like a snake. "You, however, were her first angel. How about that, Mr. Angelo? What do you make of them apples?" His laughter exploded like a repeating rocket, each boom making David flinch like a keen-eared dog on the Fourth of July.

"There, there, Mr. Angel. A sense of humor is good for the soul." Nathan pulled pieces of flesh from his forehead as he spoke, rolling them between his fingers like clay. By the time he'd flicked the tiny balls to the floor the wounds on his face had already healed.

Nathan toyed with David, putting on a show. He tormented the angel, enjoying every moment. "Say angel, is your name really Angelo or is that just a coincidence? Oh wait, I forgot. *There are no coincidences.*"

The room was truly hot now, almost like a sauna, and even though David was numbed mentally, he could still take off his coat and undo his tie, which he did methodically and without thinking.

Nathan flexed and stretched his ample form, causing his suit to tear in places. He shook his head vigorously, literally creating more hair. It spilled from his skull, a red mane down across his shoulders and back. Nathan writhed on the table over David in an almost burlesque fashion. "So, angel, how do you like the creative presentation so far?" He laughed, or was it snarled, and his shirt ripped and tore, revealing impossibly wrought muscles. You could see the tendons and feel the power.

"Excuse me, I'm here to pick up your breakfast trays." The caterer stopped speaking. She'd walked in unannounced. A diminutive, Spanish woman from an extremely devout Catholic family, she knew the Devil when she saw him. She crossed herself in the doorway, terrified.

"How about starting with the toast?" Irked by the intrusion,

Nathan destroyed her on the spot. In one blink she was a pile of dust.

Nathan exhaled in her direction, spreading the particles. "Dust to dust," he said.

Nathan regarded the spray of ashes. "Such a mess. A PR nightmare. Unless... I know! Maybe the poor woman was abducted on her way home from work. Gone missing! Perhaps I'll do something meaningless for her children. *Write a memo,*" he said, his voice dripping with malevolence. Two little spikes protruded through his hair just above the ears.

David rose up and faced the creature standing above him. "You're... *He.*"

"I've been called worse, far worse. What gave me away? My tie? Oh, I know: It's the shoes!" Nathan trotted around David, preening. The clopping sounds came not from heels but cloven hoofs.

"So you must know who I am as well?"

"Mais oui. You're the angel come to find an ad agency. God sent you." The Devil scraped the remaining clothes from his massive, sweating torso and assumed a squatting position on the table. He looked exactly like a gargoyle.

"Any more questions?"

Of course David had questions. But need he ask them? Satan held the trump card. The Devil was having his due. Oh, why had he forsaken God and come to New York? He should be in California with the agency she'd directed him to, not here. Now God's plans would be thwarted. The minute he asked himself how he could have deviated so, he realized the answer: He had succumbed to the Devil's temptation. David tried desperately to put two and two together. If the Devil was trying to ruin God's campaign, had he already sabotaged the other?

Exasperated, David cleared his throat. "Now that you've got me here, shall I assume you've already done your worst at Chloe Night?"

"Not so hard that," Nathan responded. "I merely convinced Mr. Wiener to consider my point of view."

David held his sweating head in his hands. "Wiener is a non-functioning figurehead, a recluse," he said, reiterating the comment Mila had made. "Why would his opinion even matter?" But David feared he knew the answer to that too.

"He is a majority stockholder. I get to him, I get to the company. *N'est-ce pas?*" Nathan reclined on the broad table and began scratching himself lewdly. He was in complete control and it aroused the beast.

David knew the Devil was a salacious showboat. The stories were legend. "I suppose I can understand why you would want to thwart us but why are you running an advertising agency?" he asked, depleted. "Shouldn't you be concentrating on something bigger...like infiltrating a government?"

Satan sat up and crossed his brawny legs. Smiled. "I don't know that I haven't. Who do you think gave President Clinton fellatio?" he asked, grinning like the Cheshire cat.

"Not...not Evelyn?" David shut his eyes, trying to hide his disgust. Although he didn't know the details, the focus groups in L.A. had made him vaguely aware of the former President's peccadilloes.

"Let's call her Eve, her maiden name. And come now, angel. If I'm not mistaken she was considerably more generous with you."

"But why?

"To confuse everybody. To befuddle the populace." Nathan enjoyed the topic. Evil was a lot more intellectual a pursuit than goodness. "If our heroes become sinners and our sinners saints, then whom can you trust?" The Devil brushed his hair back behind his horns. "Faith is lost."

A long time ago David partook in a Russian steam bath with his Yiddish friend from the insurance company. After five minutes his skin had felt like melting chocolate. He was sweating that way now. The Devil hadn't answered his question but David was too flummoxed to push.

"You would like to know why I have made the ad world my domain...is that not correct, Mr. Angelo?"

"Humor me, Satan. Fill in the blanks." David was weary. He was hot, defeated, and would have preferred to be back in Heaven – or failing that, out of here.

Nathan leapt off the table and got in his face. Angry at the angel's flip retort, smoke and sweat spewed from his pores. He grabbed David by the throat, hoisting him skyward, unsympathetic of his gagging.

"You think you are immortal but you're not. Know this *Angel*. I can remove you from this place as well as from Heaven. Forever. There are limbos and they are most unpleasant. There's always room for one more. Trust me." He dropped David, letting him fall like a cigarette butt.

Shocked, David could barely sit up. His neck stung something horrible. He knew he had better watch his mouth. But he also knew that in order for him to remain unscathed he'd have to keep the Devil preoccupied as well. David was afraid what Nathan would do if he suddenly got bored. Fortunately, Satan was as motivated by mental pursuits as those physical. Like a politician, the Devil enjoyed hearing himself talk. David kept pressing him.

"But why advertising?" asked David again, flinching from a pain he hadn't felt in years.

The Devil appeared to contemplate the question. He ambled over to the buffet and picked up a handful of heat-curled salmon, devouring it. With strips of warm fish dropping from his mouth Nathan responded: "Advertising makes people covet what they don't otherwise need." He nodded slowly. "There is nothing more critical to the achievement of my agenda than that....*Nothing.*"

"Your legacy has darker stains upon it than *that*. Envy and greed are flaws but they are God-given flaws...not evil." David rubbed his neck. He was as sure about what he was saying as he was sure he shouldn't be saying it.

"Not true. Every sin begins with anxiety over one's place in the world. Keeping up with the Joneses. Wish fulfillment. Coveting thy neighbor's wife. It's called motive. Murder follows. Blasphemy and all the rest."

The Devil took a crystal pitcher of ice water and poured it over his sweltering head. Steam erupted. "Man alive," he breathed. "That's the stuff!"

David considered running to the window and jumping. But he didn't know whether he still possessed any of his angelic ability, let alone if he was still immortal. Would he fall to the sidewalk like a sack of potatoes, or float serenely away?

And even if David could, where would he float? To Heaven or to one of those limbos the Devil spoke of? Nathan more than implied that David's life could be easily dispensed with. Evelyn was gone, the caterer too. From where David was sitting it appeared the Devil could do whatever the hell he wanted, literally and figuratively. He wondered why he just didn't go ahead and do it.

"Go ahead, angel. Jump. It's only 77 stories. Call it a leap of faith."

"I'm not scared. God is with me."

"How is the Lord by the way?" Nathan asked. "You know I miss her."

Nathan's dubious sincerity aside, it was still a damn good question. He wondered why God hadn't made an appearance or warned him about any of this. How could she let an innocent woman be destroyed by this monster?

"God is good. God is always good." His voice wavered.

"But?"

"We haven't communicated in a while." David answered, telling the truth. "I'm afraid my coming here was a betrayal. She's pissed off."

With a wave, the Devil summoned a bunch of grapes from the buffet. In bacchanalian fashion, he popped a few into his mouth.

"'Pissed off.' There's a phrase one doesn't usually hear in the same sentence with God, let alone coming from an angel. I like it!"

He threw the remaining grapes into the empty pitcher, turning them into wine. "Water into wine. A little trick I picked up in Sunday school. Won't you join me?"

He offered David a glass.

The last thing David wanted to do was have a drink with Satan but he couldn't very well refuse him either. Clearly Nathan enjoyed abusing all the mythological clichés associated with Christ. He'd already displayed his volatile temper. Satan was capable of anything. He brought the glass to his lips, feigning a tiny sip.

"You said you missed God. How is that?" David was not just making conversation. As odd as it sounded, Nathan's earlier statement had aroused his curiosity.

The Devil took his hand out of his pants. "Unlike you, I've known God since the beginning of my life. She once came when I called. She doted over me. She…"

Nathan stopped speaking. His ears perked up like those of a jackal. He sniffed.

"She's here."

"God?" David asked.

The steamy air below the table began moving, first subtly, then quickly picking up. It moved clockwise around the table, faster and faster, becoming a funnel. The debris on the carpet became sucked into its vortex. The hot, twirling air mass then lifted and began to revolve in an ever-tightening circle, away from the table, between them and the buffet.

David remembered an old caption from a *New Yorker* cartoon: 'Will this meeting ever end?' The picture could easily have been this. From within the tiny cyclone a figure emerged, but it wasn't God.

"That's not our Creator!" David exhorted.

"No, it's the *caterer*," Satan deadpanned.

Not whom David expected, but he was glad to see the woman alive. Without paying Nathan any mind he rushed over to her. Completely motionless and unresponsive, but she was intact. And breathing. Which meant whatever she was, she wasn't dead.

"How are you?" David beseeched.

"There's that question again," the Devil chimed, more annoyed than anything else.

Nathan began gathering the shredded fabrics that once were his suit. With hands a blur he reconstructed the garment. What was left of the steam disappeared and the room quickly assumed its original atmosphere.

"Rest assured, Mr. Angelo. She's fine. My mother has seen to that." The Devil sighed and started putting on his clothes. "Shame. I was having such a good time."

Incredulous, David spoke. "Your mother?" Saying the words made him feel naked and he began straightening his clothes as well.

The Devil tied his tie and buttoned his coat. Somehow his hair was as it was when he'd first arrived, perfectly coifed. The CEO checked himself out in the mirror then turned to face the bedraggled angel. "Haven't you figured it out yet?"

Disheveled and sweaty, David fumbled with his jacket. He didn't look like a man who could figure out which pant leg went where, let alone the Devil's mystery.

Satan smiled thinly. His teeth remained rancorous but in corporate drag he was careful not to expose them.

"God is my mother."

That was about it. The angel rushed the Devil, pushing him hard in the chest. Not expecting the attack, Nathan fell. David stood over him, enraged. "You've blasphemed enough!" David fumed. If he could have sprouted horns he would have.

The Devil got up, pushing David aside. "You were a fool to do that." He brushed himself off and faced the panting angel. "Now you really are going to meet your maker." Nathan's finger formed a menacing blade, which grew long and fierce, closing in on David's frontal lobe.

Should he fight or run? With his diminished powers David had an idea that brawling would be futile. Yet he couldn't bring himself to flee. Why he had tackled the Prince of Darkness was a riddle that he would probably take to his grave. Stepping back he said a prayer to God. He couldn't help but wonder why She hadn't come to his aid.

And then he saw the fire alarm. Pull it, David thought, and maybe, just maybe, Nathan would be forced into doing something other than killing him.

"That won't be necessary, David." God said from the four large monitors hanging from the corners. "Although I must say, I do admire your inventiveness."

"My Lord!" David spoke, falling to his knees.

The Devil froze, shooting David, and the still quiet caterer, a look that oozed death. But violence was out of the question now. One on one, God held all the cards. He sat down. While his fun might be over, God was about to learn that he had won.

God fell into the room like so many white waterfalls, each draft curling upwards upon touching the ground. She became animate, standing before them.

"You always have to make a splash, don't you, Mother?" the Devil asked. He would hold his tongue beyond that.

God ignored him, choosing to assist the stolid caterer. With a touch of Her hand the woman regained consciousness.

She immediately came to life. The caterer looked right through God, seeing only Nathan and David. She recognized the CEO. "Excuse me, Mr. Moor," she said. "I'm here to clear the breakfast."

Nathan smiled thinly and motioned to the buffet. "Very well then. See to it."

David considered the woman as she went about her business. He knew instinctively that she went to church every Sunday. He could plainly see the gold crucifix dangling from her neck. She was a good person. Her faith was unwavering. David wondered why it was God's most devout followers who were forever denied an audience with Her. It didn't seem fair. They all waited for the caterer to exit before speaking.

God spoke first. "My son has preempted me...once again."

"It is true what he says, my Lord?" the angel asked, whispering.

"Yes," God responded sadly. "And it is with a pain equal to all the strife in the world that I admit this to you."

"Oh, Mother, please."

"Hush, Lucifer!"

"The son of God is the Devil?" Myth or not, that was supposed to be Jesus Christ. Not *him*.

"My first born. Is it Nathan now?"

The Devil smirked. "I find the name change helps me win friends and influence people."

God took a palpable breath, rare for Her. "Although he is profoundly real in many people's hearts, Jesus was an early myth created to assuage the Creative Review Committee. The Creative Review Committee loathed my desire to bear a child. In their eyes it wasn't divine. And never would be. But I had the boy anyway."

David shook his head, in denial.

She stood before her son. Without asking, she removed a lock of his hair and held it to her cheek. Nathan remained silent. Like a child being punished for breaking a vase, he sat quietly in his chair, his hands folded in front of him. She continued:

"In return for my defiance, the Committee twice punished me. First by making sin a part of our world. And second, by banishing my son and provoking his rebellion. Having been presented keys to the underworld, Lucifer, a.k.a. Nathan, quickly became leader among all fallen angels. And thus, Hell was born. It was to be the opposite of Heaven and he the opposite of me."

The Devil's nails grew long and sharp. He rapaciously stuck them into his palms. He was getting restless and wanted out.

God appeared to David the same as She had when they'd visited Eden. Melancholic and wan, even her translucent hair refused to change colors. Still, David had another question: "Forgive my next query…"

"The father?" she responded, knowingly.

David nodded.

"I have no real father," the Devil snorted.

"That is only true by human terms," God stated. "For I am he as well."

Nathan grimaced as only the Devil can. He hated not having a true patriarch. He also associated women with "goodness" and thus had a hard time reconciling himself with the fact that one had created him.

David thought Her reply was both fantastic and obvious. After all, who else could it have been? He also sensed that the Creative Review Committee had had major problems with this revelation as well. Even in myth, Jesus hadn't been biologically conceived. Conception had to be immaculate. No exceptions.

God felt compelled to elaborate. David was a fine angel and had been through a lot in service to Her. He deserved answers. "I wanted to have a baby, David. I mean really have one," She said with passion in Her voice. "The ability to create life is still one of my grandest achievements. I had to feel it for myself. I hope you can understand that."

"Well, we certainly appreciate the effort," retorted Nathan snidely.

Ignoring Her son, She gazed upon the angel. "I also hope you can forgive me."

David could not believe the Lord was asking for his forgiveness. He was flattered and sad at the same time.

God turned to Nathan. "I know you've gotten to Wiener and now these people here," She said, opening her arms, implying the surroundings at T&R. "Who else have you purchased?"

Satan remained just as speechless called upon as when he'd been ignored.

This bothered David. "My Lord, I have never seen you ask a question. Do you truly not know the answer?"

"When he is not in my presence my son is but a mystery to me. It is yet another concession to the committee that I had to make.

"Who else, Nathan?" God resumed Her line of questioning.

Amused by his mother's attention, Nathan milked it by playing coy. He scratched his nose. Hesitated. From the window he pondered the view.

But God was only going to take so much of this. Her white hair began radiating light to an impossible brightness, then expressing colors like some form of psychedelic chameleon!

Fretful, Nathan spoke. "The three largest advertising concerns in the world will be mine within a year. We are already in the process of buying what few independents still remain. CN&W would be the latest acquisition."

Nathan removed a cigar from his jacket, lighting it with his finger. "So," he said, with more than a small share of arrogance, "the question isn't who else but rather who's left?"

"If only your wits served a higher purpose," God said. Small iridescent moths emerged from the corners of Her eyes.

In a day of firsts here was another: The Creator of all things was crying. David went over to God's side and stood silently in Her aura.

Satan laughed.

"So you won this battle," David shot back, holding the Lord. "Yet the world has not ended."

"He doesn't want the world to end, David," God said. "That would spoil all the fun. He merely wants it for his own." She left the angel and went over to one of the television sets.

It turned on, as did the other three, and instantly commercials began filling the room, different ones from every set. Yet were they so dissimilar? Images of pretty girls and shiny cars and bottles of beer flowed endlessly into one another, each making a case for an object or a place or a service. Drive one of these. Eat this. Fly here. Visually it was a blur. The noise became deafening.

"The world is inundated by these messages, these unholy pleas. Bombarded by them really." God spoke frankly, as if giving a business presentation. "And the world responds in kind. The desire for objects and services has become manifest." God said. "Even without Satan at the helm."

"But now I am," Nathan remarked, giddily. "Now I am!"

God continued, despite Her son. "People need to search their souls for enrichment and not the strip malls. People are craving and craving is wrong. Fine Corinthian leather is a mockery of my house. Belief in what advertisers say has become religion. Once again, my misbegotten son realized this before I did."

"The acorn, or should I say apple, does not fall too far from the tree, does it, Mother?" He snorted, reveling in his apparent victory.

"*Once again?*" David was confused.

God sighed. "In the Eighties, Lucifer permeated the corridors of Wall Street. Remember junk bonds? Yuppies? The crash of '87?"

"I also went into law," Nathan said, happy to elaborate about his conquests and achievements.

"Before my son corrupted the legal system, a lawyer was an arbiter of justice and goodwill. Now look at the profession."

"I single-handedly made the lawsuit a symbol of revenge and profiteering," the Devil beamed. Minutes before he'd been behaving like a punished child; now he was cock of the walk.

"So, now you're after Madison Avenue?" said David, catching on.

"*After?* I've already taken it." Another snort. "We've been telling people what they need, and what they want, to the point where they can't even tell the difference," retorted the Devil. "I didn't start this business, but with Town & Robertson I sure as hell am going to finish it!" Nathan pointed to the monitor closest him.

David looked up. An $80,000 sports car was zooming down a remote highway in the desert. A Gila monster followed it with his beady eyes. In the obscene world of advertising even the reptiles were materialists. Or beer guzzlers. Or both.

"Do you realize," the Devil asked, "how much time, money, and effort is put into one of those 30-second commercials?"

Nobody answered.

"Every 30-second commercial we make costs more than your average church receives in a lifetime," Satan intoned. "At T&R, we spend close to four hundred grand per spot. And we make over one thousand commercials a year. The Church and every other remaining industry of goodwill have paltry budgets by comparison, with a support structure that is feeble and weakening. People crave *things,* as they never have before. Flashy cars and ice-cold beer. Cleavage and wealth. Desire for desire's sake. Jesus walked on water. And if you buy this pair of gym shoes so can you!" Nathan forced himself to calm lest his horns appear again.

"Alas, it's true," God spoke. "In the typical American home there are an average of three television sets and the rhetoric of desire emanates from each and every one of them. During the day we see game shows that are all about money and soap operas that are all about sex..."

Nathan finished the thought, brutally: "*And then you have the adver-*

tising." The Devil methodically paced the room, resuming the presentation.

His mother seemed to be tolerating the rant, leaving David no choice but to endure it as well.

"After the six-o'clock news," Satan said, "things really go to hell. The stakes get higher. Clothes come off. Violence reigns. Cable and the Internet bring untold new avenues for sin...*and then you have the advertising.*"

If he said that one more time David was sure he'd explode. "We get it, already. We get it!" He folded his hands behind his back in order to keep his body language in check.

The Devil cared less about the angel. His mother was present and he wanted Her to see how right his reasoning was and how deft his execution. He continued his speech, boastfully: "What little time the televisions and computers are actually turned off, my gospel of greed can be readily found amongst the gaudy pages of every magazine from *People* to *Vanity Fair.*"

Satan moved his hand across the now empty credenza leaving a flow of magazines in its wake. The revelation of periodicals was bright, colorful and eye-catching; many displaying scantily clad, gorgeous women on their covers. Others objects of desire: Luxury homes. Fancy cars. Wicked gadgets. More, more, more!

"This is the number one magazine in the country," he said, picking up a shiny, thick copy of *In Style.* "In it you'll find countless stories and photographs about all the beautiful objects that all the beautiful people own. And then..."

Glumly, David finished his sentence: "*And then you have the advertising.*"

"Telling the rest of the world how and where to get theirs. And most despicably, why." The truth hurt. God's hair became darkness.

Nathan tossed the magazine up in the air. Falling, its gaudy pages came undone, cascading to the floor like dollar bills from an open Brinks truck.

"The bottom line," Nathan said, stepping on a picture of Melanie Griffith and Antonio Banderas' villa in Malibu, "is that the infrastructure of avarice and greed is well-established and continues to grow. My job, as it always has been, is to merely provide the caulking. Why bother infiltrating the radio, television and film industry when they're all brought to you by one industry...*ours?*" Nathan finally took a seat. He put his big feet up on the table. But he wasn't done preaching.

"Yes," the Devil said, taking a languid draw off of his cigar. "I have my pulpit now. It's in the living room of every home on the planet. You might say the den of iniquity is in the den."

"Enough," David said. "You've made your point. Can you not stop him, my Lord? He is your son." But David knew the answer. She would've acted by now. But surely, still, She had some options. Did not goodness always prevail...eventually?

"I cannot take any action against my son. But neither can he act against me. My notion of producing an advertising campaign to pro-mote goodness was but a reaction to what my impudent son called the growing infrastructure of avarice and greed." God spoke softly, as if these were rules that She had made and now regretted. "I'm afraid it was all part of the compromises I made at Creation. The Committee deemed an equal playing field for Good and Evil. Morals do not exist in the Universe. Only balance."

"And for that, mommy dearest, the dark side is forever in your debt." The Devil smirked.

God looked profoundly sad. David feared She might begin crying. The angel went over to the Lord, brushing by Satan. He put his arms around the woman who created him and all that he knew. "We'll find another way."

Nathan burst out laughing. "I'm touched. How come you've never hugged me like that...*Mom?*"

God lifted Her head and stared at the pitiful creature, also Her son. "The angel is right, Nathan. We will find another way...I can adapt."

And already She was changing. Her eyes and hair turned red as if erupting. Horns began to push through Her head, massive and sharp at the tip. She grew, muscles forming on top of more muscles, tendons and veins visibly rippling inside. The delicate gown She wore literally sizzled off of Her body. Her skin went mahogany. Hair sprouted from Her back thick as prairie grass. She was a he now and he opened his fanged mouth. "I can even become you!"

God spit Her tongue at Satan, knocking the cigar right out of his mouth.

Obviously, Nathan had never seen this side of his mother before and he recoiled. The Devil was speechless, his empty mouth agape.

Then the monstrously transformed being that used to be the Lord spoke:

"You really ought to do something about those teeth, son. They're disgusting." And just as quickly, God was Herself again. She even managed a smile.

"What was that?" Satan stammered. He was clearly shaken. He'd come well after the myths of Greece and Rome and so had never seen God as an instrument capable of violence.

Shocked too, David held his tongue. He didn't like observing his beloved Lord in such vile form either. On the other hand, he couldn't deny the jolt of pleasure it gave him seeing Satan blindsided like that. Anything goes, he supposed, when Heaven and Hell had a meeting.

God, more beautiful than ever, addressed Her befuddled son. "As the Chief Executive Officer of this company, would you say you have the top spot?"

"I do," replied Satan, his back straightening. Already he was regaining confidence.

"So you report to no one then?"

"I am beholden to no one...*not even you*," he hissed. His mother's bit of theater had worn off, leaving him angry. He'd won the battle. The souls of the populace were still his to manipulate. God would never have Her advertising campaign. Never. As far as he was concerned, this meeting was over. "Which reminds me," he said, "I'm a very busy man, so..."

"So, there are a few people I'd like you to meet." God walked over to the intercom, assuming the persona of Evelyn Warren.

"Evelyn?" said David.

"Eve?" said Nathan.

She engaged the speakerphone: "Naomi, will you please thank my guests for being so patient and send them into the Platinum Room. Mr. Moor will see them now."

"Evelyn?" David asked again. Yet he was too spent to even get up.

The Devil rose, indignant. "I will not see anybody, least of all your guests."

"You don't have a choice, dear boy. These people aren't merely my guests. They're your clients."

The boardroom door opened and in walked a handful of people, mostly older, well-dressed, and rich looking. Leading the way was last year's businesswoman of the year, as voted by the American Association of Advertising Agencies. Frances Elliot was the CMO of Devon Cosmetics, T&R's oldest and third largest client. She walked right up to Nathan and slapped him hard in the face.

"Frances!" the Devil exclaimed, more stunned than anything else. He was on his heels now. "What is going on here?"

"Appalled is the best word for it."

"Is something the matter?" Nathan stammered. "Did we have an appointment?"

"You're fired," she said. "Effective immediately." The stylish executive went over to Evelyn and put a hand on her shoulder. "Thank goodness your head planner here has a conscience about her. She's informed me of your escapades. If I wasn't so angry I'd be disappointed. My business is going elsewhere."

"Frances! I don't understand." Nathan was getting hot. "What did I do?"

"Oh, please, Nathan." She looked at Evelyn. "Thank you again, Evelyn, for revealing the truth. I realize the ramifications for you will be severe. But there will always be a spot for you at Devon Cosmetics. Always."

"You're most welcome," Evelyn said, keeping her head down. God played the part of company whistleblower with aplomb – humility being one of Her trademarks.

Frances gave the Devil one final glare and shook her head sullenly.

To the rest of the group she excused herself. "I have some serious public relations to tend to." And with that she left the room.

David made eye contact with Evelyn and was certain She winked at him. She was smiling, and now so was he. Indeed, God did work in mysterious ways! And this particular plan appeared to still be unfolding.

"I'm sorry, Nathan," said a portly man emerging from behind the gathering. "But I'm afraid my business will be going elsewhere as well." With his black bowler, woolen vest, and unusually curled mustache, he looked just like the Monopoly game logo. In fact, he represented an even wealthier concern. Baxter Petroleum was the largest refinery on the planet and, up until now, the agency's most lucrative client.

"I cannot have my organization associated with such...such..."

He couldn't finish his sentence. Instead he walked over to Nathan and placed both of his hands upon the large demon's shoulders. He could barely reach them. "Get help, Nathan." He tipped his hat to the others and slipped back through the crowd. He, too, gave special thanks to Evelyn.

"What goes on here?" Nathan bellowed. Frantically, he surveyed the rest of the group. Peter Weir from Ticker Toys. Shelly Blair, the CEO of Wilkenson. Even Mitchel Evans (a client whom the Devil often debauched with) was present. They represented all of T&R's biggest clients, and from each and every one of them he could see only disdain emanating from their eyes.

Desperate, the Devil ran over to Evelyn and grabbed Her. "What have you done, woman? What have you done?" He shook Her violently and Evelyn appeared to rattle in his grip. She implored him to stop but he would not. "What have you wrought?" He was screaming now, out of control.

The head of Speed Phone, a handsome, well-built, young man by the name of Kyle, pulled the Devil off of Her. "Please Nathan, you're just making matters worse."

Satan would have destroyed him with one brush of his hand but how could he, here, in front of all the others?

Mitchel rushed up and assisted Kyle subduing the fuming CEO.

"Oh please, Mitchel, don't you have some hookers waiting for you?" said Nathan, spitefully. But he refrained from fighting back. He had no choice. He hadn't trumped God. God trumped him. He'd been set up. Some serious damage control was obviously in order. And still he did not fully know what he was up against.

Evelyn straightened Her clothes and made way to the room's center. She took a deep breath, then spoke: "I did what I had to do, Mr. Moor. You were clearly operating in a conduct unbecoming a chief executive. I couldn't stand by while you, shall we say, lost your composure. Our clients deserve better."

"What 'conduct unbecoming' are you referring to, Ms. Warren?" Nathan could hardly wait for the answer.

But silently he chastised himself for overlooking such a huge vulnerability in his overall plans. *Clients.* How could he have forgotten them? Town & Robertson was a full-service agency, which meant, among other things, that they were utterly dependent upon the whims of their clients. Without them there was no company, no huge global network. And without that the Devil had no pulpit.

"You have some nerve, Mr. Moor," the Speed Phone executive retorted. "Playing dumb like this."

"Excuse me," Nathan said. He resented being talked down to by some pretty boy mortal who, he happened to know, liked boys.

"We all saw it," Mitchel said. He would've preferred not to be here at all (Nathan and he had had their share of good times) but here he was, and he had seen it, and now he had to go along.

"Saw what?" the Devil spit, trying desperately to remain calm. He hated being in the dark. If someone didn't answer his question soon he'd burst into flames. It wasn't a metaphor. He could feel the prickly heat gathering at his spine.

"This," Evelyn said, "is what everybody saw." She removed a small remote from her pocket and pressed the play button. Instantly the four monitors in the room came to life. Everybody looked up at them.

And there was Nathan, the CEO of North America's most prestigious advertising agency, pacing the boardroom and trashing the very industry that sustained him.

God turned up the volume.

All over again came Nathan's rant about a growing infrastructure of avarice and greed, and his brilliance at dominating it. "Why bother going after the radio, television and film industry when they're all brought to you by one industry...*ours.*" The part about avarice and greed was devastating.

Nathan looked at himself on the monitors – at least God had spared them his physical transformations – then back at his clients, none of whom could meet his eyes.

As Lucifer's profane speech played over and over on the hanging televisions, a procession of clients – make that former clients – made their way out the door. Evelyn shook each of their hands and apologized, promising amends and better days. These were powerful beings, but they were still mortals, and, therefore, could not see the halo of shimmering whiteness enveloping Evelyn as She saw them all off.

When they were gone, Nathan fell to his knees, sobbing.

Elated, David silently pumped his fist.

Evelyn transformed back into God. She approached her fallen son, placing a comforting hand upon his shoulder. She spoke:

"Nathan, you forgot the most elemental truth in all of creation..."

He looked up at her, helpless, drooling. "What?"

"We all report to a higher power. For an agency CEO that higher power is, and always will be, the client."

"On Earth as it is in Heaven," David whispered. He glanced at Nathan, ever so careful not to get his goat. Even vanquished, evil was still evil, still danger incarnate. Satan had been whipped but the angel knew it was only for the time being. The question wasn't whether he'd be back...it was when. Just as God was perpetual so too was Her nemesis. Whether called Lucifer, Satan, or Nathan, he was the Lord's dark shadow, a bad seed forever sprouting weeds beneath the tree of its creation.

But David couldn't help but show a smile. Goodness had prevailed; God hadn't given up. On the contrary, She'd concocted a brilliant and elaborate trap, which had caught its quarry.

Had David questioned his faith in Her? He hoped not, but to be honest, he couldn't remember. It had been such a long day. He regretted that they probably would not be doing their advertising campaign; the Devil had corrupted things so.

But he also felt content, pleased actually, and it was a joy he hadn't experienced in weeks. They wouldn't be making commercials to promote goodness but maybe, just maybe, they wouldn't have to. Perhaps some of the largest companies in the land would begin to look harder at what their agencies were doing.

The white light surrounding God grew stronger, filling the room.

Anything was possible.

EPILOGUE

"**T**HIS is one of my favorite places in the world, David." The wind was blowing very hard and God's hair rippled colorfully into it like a flag. "It's a shame they don't allow people up here anymore," She said. "There are few views that show off humankind's potential for greatness as well as this one." They were on the old viewing platform atop the Statue of Liberty's torch. It was just the two of them.

Some gray gulls were riding the heavy gusts above. Occasionally, one would call out but they seemed not to have an agenda.

As a small child, David had been one of the thousands of immigrants entering into the New World. Where they were standing now towered above him then. Lady Liberty had been a great shepherd calling in her flock. Brand new at the time, it gleamed like a heavenly being.

Now, of course, it was grimy and corroded as would be expected of a metal object surrounded by water and the elements. Still, the view from her was, if anything, more magnificent now than ever. David watched as a helicopter headed down to one of the metropolis's many heliports.

"I was here when they put Lady Liberty up," God said, unprovoked. "October 1886. It was quite the undertaking. Photography was in its infancy but I recall seeing as many of them as painters marking the occasion." God's eyes were shut as She spoke. But as always, She was seeing.

David realized how much Her visage resembled that of the statue and he wondered seriously if it was a coincidence.

But there are no coincidences!

And then he remembered a summer day in another era and he, too, shut his eyes...

Word of their arrival into port had traveled quickly through the cramped vessel. And David had been among the first to claw his way up from steerage to take in the New World.

He kicked opened the doors to daylight fully expecting to see Heaven. He was not disappointed for when he looked up it was as if he saw God. The Statue of Liberty lorded above them, as grandiose and regal as anything he'd ever seen, even in Rome. His younger brother had come up behind him and so they stood, arm in arm, beholding her, attributing the sun on their faces to her, the salty spray, the scent of land. Praying for their new life and for the first time, in a long time, feeling good about their prospects.

"That's right, David," God said, feeling his memory as vividly as Her own. "This Lady was as good as a God to many people. She symbolized rightness that for them had never existed." With gravity God added: "On my best days I can only hope to accomplish as much."

The Lord opened Her eyes and two small tears tumbled into the harbor. The drops were like the silver fish one sees in dreams – elusive, shiny, and slippery. Both watched as the droplets vanished into the murky water below. Two small rainbows remained, giving evidence of their path. But, they too, quickly dissipated, victims of the harbor's blustery atmosphere.

"Nothing remains, dear boy. All my rainbows disappear."

"But they were beautiful and inspirational," replied David.

God turned to Her beloved, chosen angel. She smiled. "That, as mortals are wont to say, is the kicker. I always make an impression but it seldom sticks. Only faith remains, if it remains."

"But faith is everything, my Lord," David responded. "And it does remain!"

"And so this is where our little saga began, Mr. Angelo, is it not?"

David had to apologize. "I'm sorry, but I'm not following you."

"It wasn't many 24-hours ago, we were in a temple not too far from this very spot, and you told me that faith was not only our best ally but, ultimately, our only ally. Remember? You argued quite passionately."

David did, but he was surprised at how long ago it seemed.

In fact, it had been a few days.

God took to the air, falling into formation with the hovering seagulls. "You scoffed at my idea about soliciting an advertising agency to promote my agenda…to promote goodness…in all of its forms."

She rolled and twirled between the flock of birds.

If the gulls were aware their creator was among them they certainly weren't showing it. The wind was right, affording them little need to exert precious energy. Soon the fishing boats would be in with their bounty of heads and entrails. What need did they have of God?

"Maybe you were right," God said. She alighted upon the iron rail of the viewing stage, surefooted as a bird. Her hair shimmered like mother of pearl.

"Maybe?" He wasn't questioning his previous opinion. It was God's lack of conviction that surprised him. If She wasn't sure about a thing then what was there to be sure about at all?

"Join me, David." God drifted backward over the ocean, opening her arms.

David wrinkled his brow, contemplating the chasm between where he was standing and the cold waters below.

"Forgive me for not leaping, my Lord," he said tentatively. "It's just that I've lost confidence in my angelic powers. Back in that boardroom I'm afraid I was as helpless as any mortal."

"With faith mortals are never helpless. I won't let you down," She continued, smiling tenderly, sensing his insecurity. "Come, ye of little faith!"

David gazed up at his Creator and suddenly this warmth came over him, belying the chilly environs. He felt loved in a way he'd ever experienced before, not from his wife and certainly not from Evelyn. Even a mother's love paled. He couldn't believe that Nathan, or anyone really, had rejected such a feeling. He couldn't fathom why or, given how powerful the sensation, even how.

One last time David admired the Statue of Liberty. She represented freedom. Freedom to pursue happiness. Freedom to dream. And freedom to believe in God.

Returning to his Creator, God offered the possibility of love, as She always did, as She was now.

Like any mortal he had the freedom to choose Her love.

Would that have made a good slogan? **Choose Love.**

At that moment, David realized even had they been able to advertise, it probably would not have worked.

For he *had* been right. While there were countless ways to sell people on the virtues of goodness and love, without faith in that path leading somewhere special few would believe, let alone take it.

In God we trust.

For shame, David had to die and go to Heaven and come back again before confirming what he'd known all along!

But his regret was fleeting. Maybe it never existed at all.

David leapt off the balcony into God's open arms, the wind rushing by him like memories, jingles from another life and time.

THE END

AUTHOR'S NOTE

WHILE writing this book it came to my attention that there was an outdoor campaign running in the Southern states supposedly created by God! The clever messages told people – in no uncertain terms – to get religion *or else.* If I remember correctly one went as follows:

What part of *Thou shalt not* don't you understand?
– God

It would be easy enough to discover the name of the "actual" author of this beguiling campaign but I chose not to. However, I would like to wish the creator luck in his *or her* mission as well as in the advertising award shows!

Finally, I thank you, the reader, for having given this book your time, and I sincerely hope you will ask others to do the same.

God bless.